ALPHA'S VOW

RENEE ROSE
LEE SAVINO

Midnight
ROMANCE

WANT FREE BOOKS?

ALPHA'S VOW

The sweet human is pregnant with my pup.

We had one night together, and then she ghosted. Apparently, I'm not part of her 'life plan'.

Whatever, angel. Plans change.

She thinks I'm a player. That I won't stick around. She thinks I don't have what it takes to be a dad.

That I won't drop everything and dedicate my life to our baby. To our family. To her.

She's wrong. She thinks I'll walk away?

She has no idea what she's in for. A wolf never walks away from his mate, and he always protects his pups.

I may not have marked her yet, but I will.

And if she tries to run, I'll follow.

I'll hunt my beautiful female to the ends of the Earth.

CHAPTER 1

harlie

THE BEST THING about hiking down to the hot springs at six-thirty in the morning is that no one else will be there. Manby Hot Springs—the three rock pools near the ruins of an old stagecoach bathhouse—can get crowded with naked hippies, both local and visiting, but not on a weekday. Not at this time of day. And definitely not when it's snowing.

The sun is just starting to rise behind Taos Mountain, painting the sky in shades of pink, purple and orange. That, and the gentle snowflakes, feel like a perfect birthday gift from nature.

This hike is my own present to myself. I have to work in a couple hours, but I don't want my birthday to consist of nothing but delivering mail. I want to do something to set it apart. I'm getting together with my friends for drinks in the plaza later, but soaking in the hot springs at sunrise seems like a great way to make the day special.

And get my mind off Chad.

My baby brother is serving over in Afghanistan, and hasn't been heard from for months. Not even our parents—both retired Air Force officers—have been able to get a message to or from him.

Official word from the Air Force is that no news is good news, but I've had this low-level fear for him ever since he enlisted and it's starting to get noisier. It's probably unfounded. I'm a worrier in general, and I'm probably just fixating on this, but I sure would feel better if he would just let us know he's alive.

I reach the end of the one-mile hike into the canyon that dead ends at the edge of the Rio Grande, and strip out of my clothes. I tuck them behind a rock because the neat freak in me doesn't want to look at them while I'm basking in nature. It's also why I prefer to come here alone. Other people don't help me commune with nature, and they just mess with the landscape.

The softly falling snow means it's actually warmer than usual, and there's no cold wind. The hot water is going to feel heavenly. I take my time, stepping in slowly, savoring the contrast of the hot water surrounding my legs and the cold prickling my skin everywhere else.

I sink into the steam, settling my bare ass on the soft black sand so I can get my shoulders completely under water.

Across the river, on the slope of the opposite canyon wall, a movement catches my eye and I draw in a pleasured gasp.

A giant bighorn sheep turns his head to stare at me.

"Hey there, big guy." I lift my hand in a wave, smiling. "Thanks for dropping in."

He lowers his head to graze.

Satisfaction flows through me as I drink in the stillness. I sink even lower until the water covers my ears and chin and I close my eyes, enjoying the way the heat seems to soak into my bones.

And then I nearly jump out of my skin when a body plunges into the shallow pool from the rocks above. I stare at the chaos of water and body parts, trying to make sense of it. Somehow, impossibly, it takes the shape of a man—an extremely fit, *naked* man—who stands and stares back, seemingly as shocked as I am to not find himself alone.

For a moment, my brain short circuits. He's insanely ripped—as if God invented some extra muscles for him. Either that, or he has more than his quota. Maybe there are people running around this Earth with muscles missing because this guy took them all. If so, then one of those people is me.

I sink a little lower in the water.

"Hi."

That's the only thing I can think to say to the magnificent, dripping specimen of manhood. I grew up as a military brat. I've seen enough shirtless man-chests to inoculate me against the appeal. But this guy's tattooed pectoral glory might be the exception.

"Hey." He attempts to cover his manhood with both hands, and backs up. I recognize him—he's one of the ex-military guys Sadie's boyfriend works with. The mercenaries. Huge guys. Muscled. Dangerous.

Super hot.

I grin at his attempts to be a gentleman. I think my presence startled him even more than he startled me. "You can come in. And you don't have to cover up. Nudity is expected down here."

His eyes crinkle and he smirks, turning slightly to shield me from the sight of his peen. Of course, that gives me a delicious view of his epic, muscled backside. "Yeah, sorry, but this gun is fully loaded for you."

Oh. "Um, thanks?"

He laughs softly and walks toward me, dropping to his knees to hide said *gun* under the steam. I'm now oddly disappointed I didn't get to see it.

"My bad. I never would've jumped in if I'd known someone was in here. I'm Lance." He holds out his hand.

"Charlotte. My friends call me Charlie." When I reach to take his palm, my shoulders come out of the water. His gaze dips to the place where my breasts emerge from the steaming surface. He inhales sharply, his nostrils flaring. His ocean blue eyes lock onto my face. The lazy heat in his eyes warms me all over.

Damn, but he's beautiful. And the way he's looking at me... his obvious appreciation revs my sex drive. The one that stalled after experiencing Taos' very limited range of dating possibilities... after realizing The Big Plan I had for my life might never come together.

"No worries," I say. "You just surprised me."

His grin has a hint of a dimple. *Yowza.* Face of a model, charm of a movie star, the sleekly muscled shoulders of an Olympic swimmer. Triple threat. "What are you doing here all by yourself at sunrise, Charlie?" he purrs. The question shouldn't sound like he just offered me sex, but for some reason, it does. He floats closer, hovering right at the edge of my personal bubble.

And I tilt my head up at him with a smile, ready to flirt with him even though I shouldn't. This guy has *player* scrawled across his muscled chest. I've met a million guys like him on base, where I grew up. Military playboys who fuck anything with a pulse, and don't ever look back.

Not to be judgmental, but I know his type. Fun to date,

but here one day, ghosting the next. The opposite of the type I need for The Big Plan.

And yet here I am, savoring his charm like it's my favorite mocha shake, complete with chocolate sauce, whipped cream, and shavings of dark chocolate on top.

"It's my birthday," I find myself saying, even though I didn't plan on telling anyone who didn't already know.

Lance flashes a lady-killer grin. "Happy birthday, Charlie." He murmurs my name like he's savoring it.

If he were any other guy, I'd roll my eyes and put up my usual defenses. I could still shrug Lance's charm off. If I told him to stay away, he would. But he's floating naked in the water, so close, so gorgeous, his attention all on me. It feels like fate.

"If we were at a bar, I'd buy you a drink. But since we're naked in a hot spring, would you accept a back rub?" His dimple makes an appearance. This Charm Boy's got a license to kill—with those long lashes, sculpted cheekbones, and baby blues. "A birthday massage?"

Ha. There it is. He's playing his role as player so perfectly, it could be scripted. But fuck it, I want to let it happen.

"How about a foot rub?" I challenge, and let one foot drift up in the water between us.

He doesn't falter. He claims my foot, keeping it under water and stroking his thumbs along my arch. He's good. Infinitely skilled. He uses just the right amount of pressure between the long metatarsal bones, rolls and pulls each toe like he's uncorking a bottle of fine wine. And then he starts working between my toes.

My plan has backfired. Every point he presses on my foot sends pleasure shooting up between my legs. This is foreplay.

Aw, damn. This guy is so hot, he's going to make the

water in this pool boil. If I didn't know fifty things about screwing military guys, I'd do him. Not to incorporate him into The Big Plan. God, no. Just for fun. Just for me.

I know he'd be good in bed.

"You're friends with Sadie," he observes.

I blink. I shouldn't be surprised he remembers that—we've met once before, briefly, in a restaurant. He just seems like the kind of guy who doesn't notice anyone but the girl who's naked and right in front of him.

"You're friends with Deke," I counter.

His amusement seems to grow. He studies me with those dimples flexing. "You wear cute t-shirts."

I should not be so pleased he noticed. He *does* know me. And he likes my shirts. Or thinks they're cute—is that the same thing?

"You ride a Harley."

He shakes his head. "Ducati." Then he shrugs, like he realizes I probably don't care to hear the difference. "Yeah."

Okay, I like this guy. I don't want to, but he's really hard not to like. Especially when he's working between my toes like he knows it's somehow the secret path north, straight between my legs.

For one insane moment, I consider jumping him right here in the hot spring pool. But I don't do spontaneous. Ever. Nothing happens in my life without a thorough think-through. Without a plan.

"I heard you're Special Forces."

A hint of wariness creeps into his gaze. His face becomes little guarded. That makes sense. Special Forces is serious. He probably did and saw things that changed him forever. That's what I'm afraid of for Chad.

But I guess that's what he wanted—Chad, that is, not Lance. He knew what he was getting into when he enlisted.

6

"Was," Lance says, and the serious tone in his deep voice does things to my insides that rivals the pleasure from his touch. "We're in private security now."

Right. I knew that, too, and I'm not sure how I feel about it. Special forces have skills that translate to mercenary work in the private sector. Tough, dangerous work that pays real well. I've seen their fancy cars and bikes. They're *rolling* in cheddah. Private contracts are lucrative, but dangerous as hell. And I have a feeling that what Lance and his buddies do may not be entirely legal.

Either way, Lance is a grade-A adrenaline junkie. He left the military, but couldn't leave the life. Nothing wrong with that, but not a guy I could see myself with.

I point at my chest. His eyes track the movement like a tiger watches his prey. "Military brat. Both parents were active duty and deployed a lot."

His expression softens. "Sorry?"

I laugh. "Yes. Thank you. I'm definitely scarred from it."

He works my heel, pinching all around the circumference, then stroking up my Achilles. My nipples stiffen despite the hot water. I make a mental note not to lift my shoulders above the waterline to let him see his effect on me.

"The moving around, or the deployments? Which branch?"

He succeeds in disarming me a little more every minute I remain here with him. His question shows he gets it, and the way he watches me for my answer makes it seem like he's really interested.

He's interested in getting laid, my snarky side reminds me.

"Both. Both my parents were Air Force. We moved a lot, and if my parents were deployed at the same time, we stayed with my grandparents. Different school almost every year."

Lance's gaze is sympathetic.

"But no, I don't have a problem with the military culture, *per se.*"

He quirks a brow and his hand strokes sensuously up the calf of my other leg until it catches the heel and he changes which foot he's massaging. My pussy clenches. This guy has *all* the moves. He starts to stroke my other foot, and I stifle a groan of pleasure.

"You live in Taos. Isn't the culture here the polar opposite?"

I laugh. "Good point. Why did you guys choose here?"

"I asked you first."

I swear to God, my nipples hum with pleasure. This man has every nerve ending in my body tingling for him. "Okay, you're right. I picked Taos because I wanted the opposite of what I had growing up. I wanted a place to put down roots and stay forever. And I love Taos. It's beautiful, and I like the liberal vibe here. But I'm not a hippie. I'm not a fly-by-night just passing through until Spirit sends me somewhere else."

"No." His gaze is warm. "You seem pretty grounded."

Compliments. Another technique in the playboy manual. Lance is smoother than most guys, I'll give him that. I need to make my escape before I have no defenses left. Actually, I need to leave, anyway, if I'm going to get to work on time. I already stayed much longer than I planned.

"Yes, well, as much as I'm loving this, I need to get out. I have to be at work by eight."

Lance drops my foot and launches himself to his feet, dripping water. He turns to angle his hips away from me. Does he still have a hard-on?

"Right." He's already climbing out of the pool, giving me that epic view of his smooth ass. Water streams in rivulets between the powerful muscles of his quads, shoulders, and back.

I can't speak for a moment. It's like viewing fine art, a marble sculpture of a Greek god. There are no words.

"Give me a head start, and I'll leave you in private to get out and dressed."

Such a gentleman. Anyone less suave would hang around and try to sneak a few peeks. Offer to walk with me up the canyon.

His cheek curves as he tosses over his shoulder, "Happy birthday, Charlie. I hope to see you again soon."

He disappears around behind the ruins of the old bath-house, away from the trail that leads out of the canyon. And then, I could swear it sounds like he's running.

I climb out of the pool, curiosity winning out over any fears I have of flashing him, but he's disappeared. I scan the trail up the side of the canyon.

No sign of him.

What... the heck?

Where did he go? And why was he in such a hurry? It doesn't make sense, but I don't have time to worry about it. If I don't throw on my clothes and hoof it out of here, I'll be late for work.

Lance

RAFE WOULD KILL me if he knew about my cock-up.

And I don't mean the boner I sprouted for the stunning human.

Charlie.

The girl whose face I'll be jerking off to every night this week.

I race along the river in wolf form, trying to put some distance between me and the hot spring pool before Charlie climbs out to discover that I don't have any clothes to put on —oh, and I happened to swim there from the John Dunn bridge. *In wolf form.*

The cold snow-water river dunk followed by a dip in the hot spring has been my latest indulgence. Today was the third morning I'd ridden my Ducati down to the low bridge, stripped out of my clothes, and swum with four legs downstream in the icy water to then shock my system with the pleasure of the hot spring. It is a totally unsanctioned activity, since showing our wolves anywhere near humans is forbidden.

But damn, it feels so good. The contrast of freezing cold and then steaming hot. The early morning exhilaration of exercise and pleasure.

But I can't risk it again. I don't know how my wolf didn't pick up on Charlie's presence before I launched into that pool.

Fuck!

I was in wolf form when I jumped. I literally had to shift mid-air when I realized she was in there.

I'm so fucking lucky her eyes were closed and she didn't see my wolf.

I was flustered by my mistake, and then by her scent, which was alluring, but hard to catch in the water. It drove me wild trying to get the full notes of it. Like pine and peaches rolled into one.

I've seen Charlie in town before. She's in that group of females that hangs out with Deke's mate, Sadie. But today was the first time I got close enough to smell her, and now I crave more. A lot more.

Maybe it's just the fact that she was naked and I'd just shifted, but I sprouted a chub that refused to go down the entire time I was in that pool with her. I mean, I'm the kind of guy who appreciates a naked female, regardless of her scent. Any naked female.

Maybe it's been too long since I've managed to get a female in bed, because while I didn't see that much of Charlie, the thoughts about what she was hiding under all that steam and water nearly drove me wild.

I definitely want to see more of her.

All of her. Preferably writhing underneath me, screaming my name as I make her come.

Maybe tonight. It is her birthday, after all. It would be a shame to leave a woman unsatisfied on her birthday. But Rafe would cut my dick off if I did hunt her down to make her scream. We're not supposed to fraternize with civilians— a.k.a humans. Charlie's friends with Sadie, which means things could get messy. Living in a small town makes it nearly impossible to screw around.

I arrive at the low bridge where I left my Ducati. After lifting my nose to scent the air for humans, I shift back to my two-legged form, emerge from the brush, and change into my clothes by my bike.

What Rafe doesn't know won't hurt him.

harlie

"Happy birthday!" Adele throws her arms around me. I was so absorbed in my thoughts and my martini, I didn't even hear her approach.

"Shhh, keep it down," I say, even as I hug her back. "I don't want the whole restaurant to know. The staff might come out and sing."

"Don't worry, they don't do that here. I even called the manager to make sure."

"Oh good. Thank you. I still have nightmares about last year." We went to a Mexican restaurant, and Tabitha got the whole Mariachi band to play birthday songs for fifteen straight minutes.

"So do I." Adele lifts a giant bag filled with white and gold chocolate boxes onto the table beside me. My mouth waters at the sight. The only thing better than a best friend who owns a chocolate shop is being a guinea pig for all her new chocolatey concoctions. "The whole restaurant is under strict instructions to not make a big deal. But I can't promise Tabitha won't circumvent me and hire a stripper."

"Oh, God." I try to imagine a male stripper and immediately think of Lance. Shirtless, that wolf tattoo swaying to music, a cocky smile on his face. I choke on my drink, and sputter.

Adele thumps my back. "You okay?"

"Fine. Wrong tube." I have got to get a hold of myself. "What's new with you? How's The Chocolatier?"

A distressed look flashes over Adele's face before she smoothes it out. "Let's not talk about work," she says. "What about you? Did you do anything special today?"

"Just work." And hot tubbing with a hottie. Nekkid. My cheeks flush. I turn my head and rest my chin in my hand, trying to hide it, but Adele knows me too well.

"Nu-uh, that's not the whole story. What happened?"

"There may have been a hot guy involved."

"Oooh," she gasps. "Not a stripper?" she teases.

"Nope." I duck my head close to her. "And don't tell anyone else." I love all my friends, but I don't want everyone knowing I think Lance is hot. Then Sadie would get excited and try to hook us up on double dates or something, and I'm not about to go out with the guy. Lance is not part of The Big Plan.

"Secret's safe with me. What's he like?"

I roll my eyes. "He's a player. I can tell. Like every fly-boy on base growing up." I push my martini away. "But he wants in my pants, and I definitely considered it for a minute."

The waitress comes by, and Adele orders a bottle of wine for the table before turning back to me. "So? Why not jump him?"

I gape at her. I'd expect Tabitha, our hippie friend with no real job and a strict *laissez faire* code, to advocate free love and one-night stands, but not Adele. We all look up to Adele, not because she's a year older, but because she's so responsible and put together. She runs her own business and spends every waking minute in full make up and tasteful high heels, looking ready for a photo shoot in Paris. She's the only person I know who regularly accessorizes with scarves.

"It's not part of The Big Plan," I say.

"Right." Adele loosens her pretty cream-colored neck scarf and smooths back a perfect brown curl. "What's the plan again?"

I take a deep breath. "Marry by thirty, have two point five kids. Raise them in Taos, but travel and hike a different national park each summer. Retire at fifty."

"Hmmm." Adele narrows her green eyes at me.

"Once I'm retired, I might do something crazy," I add, so I don't seem too boring. "Like start a cactus farm. Or cross-breed different varietials of ficus."

The waitress delivers the wine. Adele pours a glass and takes a healthy sip. "All right, you want my advice?" She sets the glass down with a thump. "Forget the plan. You spend your whole life working for something, only to have it fail. You might as well set it on fire and toast marshmallows."

My jaw drops to my lap. "Okay, what is going on with you? Did something happen? Is it the shop?"

"I don't want to talk about it." There are grooves around her mouth I've never noticed before. "Not on your birthday. Today is about you. And I think you should do it. Sleep with him, whoever he is. Not as part of the plan; just to enjoy a hot man. Get it out of your system."

The rest of our friends arrive, and Adele sits back with a placid smile, no sign of her earlier stress. I let her deflect attention onto me, but make a mental note to check on her later.

As for her advice, well... maybe I can add a one-night-stand addendum to The Big Plan. One night doing the horizontal tango to get Lance out of my system. *Wham, bam, thank you, military man.* Then he'll move on, and I'll get back to searching for someone with long term potential. Someone who's husband material. Maybe I can find someone with an accounting background, so every year he can do our taxes.

My plan is perfect. What could go wrong?

Lance

Working in intelligence has its perks. Without resorting to asking Deke—which would show my hand—I find out everything I can about Miss Charlie. Where she works—the U.S. Post Office; where she lives—her own little adobe house in town; and, most importantly for tonight's plan—the make, model of her car. How else will I be able to casually bump into her on her birthday?

She has to be going out with her friends.

It doesn't take me long to do a drive-by of the restaurants in the Taos area, and I finally spot her Subaru Forester beside Sadie's white Hyundai in front of the nicest restaurant in Arroyo Seco.

I don't go in. She's with her friends. It would be awkward. Instead I go full recon, parking my bike across the street under a tree, slouching down in my seat and watching through tinted windows. A full blown stakeout. Something I've done many times, but never, ever for a woman.

But Charlie's different. My wolf assures me she's special.

16

And I'm going to find out why.

When the pack of females emerge, I get out, stealthily cross the street, and then seem to appear from the side street, casually passing near Charlie's car. "Hey, birthday girl."

She draws in her breath and swivels her hip to lean against her car. "Lance."

Oh fuck. I like the way my name sounds on her lips. I catch her peach-pine scent—her full scent this time without the water to wash it away—and it hits me square in the nuts. My jeans get way too tight.

Damn. I haven't had this strong a reaction to any female before—human or shifter. I move my hips, trying to lessen the pressure, but otherwise ignore the bulge down below, hoping she won't look down and notice.

"I'm here to buy you that drink." It's a line. I've used them on women before, but I'm not usually so attached to the outcome. For some reason, it matters that she'll say yes to me.

She hesitates, her gaze flicking to her friends, getting in their cars. They don't notice that I'm here. They're already back in their own little bubbles.

"Just one drink." I switch on the charm, practicing that effect I mastered of making my interest seem casual, friendly, and non-threatening. It comes in handy on missions. I'm the guy they send in as distraction. I have a face people think they can trust, a face that hides the power and ferocity of the animal that lurks beneath the surface. It's the opposite of the intimidating vibe my brother—our alpha—Rafe goes for. Or the giant, leather-clad Deke, our biggest pack member.

Of course, I'm not a threat. Not to Charlie.

Just to her panties.

Charlie considers me, wisps of her blonde bob falling across her face. She knows I want in said panties. I get the feeling she knows exactly what I am, minus the wolf part. I doubt I'm her type, but I'm familiar. She grew up on bases with guys like me all around her. So she's thinking about it. It's her birthday, after all. And after that foot rub, she probably knows that I can make her feel good.

She drags her plump lower lip through her teeth, debating. "One drink," she agrees.

My wolf fist pumps the starry night sky. I touch her back lightly and lead her back into the restaurant, where we sit at the bar. She takes her turquoise puffy winter coat off. She's in one of her graphic t-shirts under a cropped jacket. This one is of a rainbow unicorn dabbing. The shirt fits tight and small, accentuating her narrow waist and perky tits. She dressed the outfit up with a pair of high-heeled boots under her dark blue jeans.

I have to stop the wolf-like growl of approval that rises up in my throat.

The bartender is a pretty twenty-something with long red hair up in a ponytail. I make a mental note that she's hot, and add her to my possibility list, but as soon as I have the thought, my wolf shuts it down.

Charlie, he growls.

Yeah, I know. I'm working on Charlie. The redhead would be for later.

My wolf still isn't having it. Charlie's peachy-pine scent is wreaking havoc on both of us. I want to skip the drinks and throw her up against the closest wall. Bury my cock so deep in her, she never looks at another man again.

Which is… inappropriate. I thought I was supposed to be the suave one. I'm feeling as feral as Deke was before he found Sadie.

"I'll have a dirty martini," Charlie tells the pretty bartender. I resist making an innuendo about the *dirty* part, especially when I see her gaze slide over to me like she's waiting for it. Instead, I just wink. "Gray Goose and tonic for me." I put my back to the bar, settling my full attention on Charlie. "Did you get a birthday treat tonight?" Okay, there might have been innuendo in that question.

Charlie's gaze drops to my lips for a moment, like she's considering where her treat might come from.

That's right, beautiful. This mouth can make you scream.

"I, um, did, yes." Her hands slow in the act of taking off her cropped jacket. I've flustered her. Or her own thoughts have. A light flush spreads up her neck. "The flourless chocolate torte. Adele, Tabitha, and Sadie helped me eat it."

"Good," I rumble. "Birthday girls should get all the treats."

"Yes." Her nipples are protruding through her t-shirt and bra. She's picking up what I'm laying down. Our drinks come and Charlie takes a healthy sip from hers, like she's trying to steady herself. Or maybe she's dulling her resistance to me. I can scent her arousal. She knows what I'm offering and she wants it. She just isn't sure yet if she's going to let herself have it.

I don't touch my drink. My mission is not even close to complete.

"Has it been a good one so far?"

"My birthday?" Charlie considers. "I had a nice morning, even though some guy came and belly flopped into the hot spring right next to me." She's teasing. Oh Fates, she's teasing. That's a good sign.

"Oops," I deadpan. "What an asshole."

"It's okay, he made up for it," she murmurs almost too low for me to hear.

I grin bigger. "Good. I'm sure he'll never do it again. Of course, he might have noticed you were in there if you hadn't hidden your clothes under a rock."

She laughs. "You found them, huh?"

I lean closer and dip my head to her ear. "I didn't think you hiked there nude." Her breath hitches when I say the word *nude* and I lean back to continue, "I was looking when I climbed out, to figure out where I went so wrong. I usually have far better recon skills than that."

A shadow passes over her face. If Charlie were any other woman, I'd ignore it or distract her until I can get her in bed. But I can't with Charlie. She matters to me—even though we've just properly met.

I review my words to figure out what triggered her. I know from my research that her parents are both still alive and together, retired from active duty and living in Green Valley, Arizona.

"What are you thinking about?" I ask softly.

"Oh. Um, *recon*." She fingers her drink, falling silent like she expects me to move on. But I keep silent, waiting, so she gives a little nod and continues, "I was thinking about my brother. He's currently deployed and I haven't heard from him for six months. It's driving me nuts."

Chad Holland, age twenty-four, active duty Air Force. I haven't dug into his information beyond that. "You're worried about him."

She nods. "I'm sure he's fine. My mom keeps saying she's sure he's fine." She rubs her temples. "I grew up always worrying one or both of my parents weren't going to make it home every time they were on tour. You'd think by now I would've learned how to stop it."

I brush a lock of blonde hair that strayed across her face. "How to stop worrying?"

"Yeah."

"My brother's the one who worries in our family." I flash her a rueful smile. "I think he figures if he does it all, I won't have to."

She looks under her lashes at me. There's no mascara on them. Like this morning, her face is natural and fresh. Beautiful. "You seem pretty relaxed."

I shrug. "Like I said, Rafe takes all the responsibilities on his shoulders."

"So you're the playboy."

Ouch. I shouldn't be offended. She's right, I am the playboy. At least where women are concerned. The label fits, but tonight I don't like it. I want Charlie to think better of me.

I take her drink from her hand and set it down. "I'm the playboy who knows how to make you forget your worries for one night, birthday girl. Will you let me?"

Her eyes darken and she draws in a shaky breath. "Um…"

"I'll let you ride my Duck."

"Your Duck?" She wrinkles her nose. "Is that some sort of euphemism?"

I deepen my voice and deliver the line with a cheesy seductive flair. "Only if you want it to be."

She shakes her head, rolling her eyes.

"My Ducati," I clarify. "Duck, or Duke, if you prefer."

"Mmm. I've never ridden a Duck before." Her tone is sultry, and she overdoes it by fluttering her eyelashes at me. "Or a Duke."

Wowza. Even when she's fake-flirting, she's over-the-top sexy. "I'll even let you drive."

She laughs. "What makes you think I want to?"

"I know you want to." I toss a few bills on the bar to cover our drinks.

Her smile is miraculous. It makes my wolf preen at

having coaxed it out of her. "Wow."

"Let's go." I stand and grab her jacket from the back of the chair.

She rises and I hold her jacket out for her, then rest my hand on the small of her back. It fits perfectly, like it was made to ride there. I lead her outside and pull the keys to the Ducati from my pocket. "Have you driven a motorcycle before?"

She draws in a long breath and exhales. "Not since high school."

"It's easy. Like riding a bike. If you've done it once, you won't forget." We arrive at my bike. "Don't be nervous."

She darts a glance at me, then back at the bike. "Are you going to ride with me?"

"Of course, angel. I'll be with you the whole way." I pause. "Unless you want me to follow you in your car?"

"No, I want you on the bike. Definitely. I don't want to do this alone."

I zip her puffy jacket up to her chin and put my helmet on her head, tightening the chin strap. She pulls a slim pair of brown leather gloves from her pockets, and puts them on. Reaching past her, I put the keys in the ignition. "Go ahead. Climb on." I quirk a smile.

"Oh boy. This is crazy," she says, but throws her leg over like a pro and grasps the handlebars. "This one is the clutch. This one is the brake. Right?"

"Exactly." I take every opportunity to touch her, closing my fingers over hers to make sure her grip is good, running a hand down her back over her coat to soothe her.

"This is nuts," she repeats, finding the button to turn on the headlight. "I must be crazy."

"You're fine. I'll be right here." I mount the bike behind her. Her small body is wedged between my legs, her bottom brushing my cock. Her peachy-pine scent surrounds me, and I savor the moment. Just being close to her, I could die happy.

"Okay, I'm remembering how this goes."

I reach around to rest my hands over hers on the handlebars. "You've got this."

"The gears are down here?" She finds the pedal on the left.

"Yep."

"Okay." She blows out her breath. "Here goes nothing." She kickstarts the motorcycle and it roars to life. "Maybe I do remember how to do this," she mutters, as if to herself.

She squeezes the clutch closed and shifts to first, then gives it a little gas and lets out the clutch. We move forward smoothly.

"Perfect." I let go of the handlebars to rest my hands lightly on her thighs. Enough contact to prime her for what's coming. Not enough to distract her from driving.

She takes it slow at first, following the curving road back toward town. When it opens up into a long, straight stretch, she lets her speed climb. I hear her exhilarated laugh filter back on the wind, along with that delectable scent.

I want to bury my face in her hair and bite her neck. It's a strange thought—not one I usually have with females, especially not the human variety. I've never had the urge to mark a female before, but the desire seems present tonight.

Maybe because I'm approaching thirty. My wolf wants me to mate.

Sorry, not gonna happen, buddy.

Relationships are forbidden in our little pack. At least, they were until Deke met Sadie, his mate.

Charlie slows down when we get into town, stopping at the first light. I put one leg down to lean on so she doesn't have to.

"Having fun?" I call out over the wind.

"Yes." She sounds excited, like she almost can't believe she decided to do this. The music of it seems to fall all around me, tiny shards of pleasure piercing my skin.

The light turns to green, and she puts the bike in gear and slowly takes off, finding her way into town and stopping in front of a small house on a quiet back street.

"This is my place."

I reach around her to turn the bike off.

"I guess you think you're coming in." There's laughter in her voice.

"I'm coming in," I tell her. "I have a job to do."

"Oh yeah?" She's flirting now, something I would guess is out of character for her. "What's that?"

"My job is to make you scream until you're hoarse, sweetheart." I unfasten the helmet from her chin and take it off. "And I plan to take my time, so we'd better get started if you want to sleep at all tonight." I wink.

She hesitates, even though we both know she's already made her decision. "Does this work on every woman?"

"I don't try it on every woman. You are the only woman I've ever let drive my motorcycle," I tell her. It's the truth. Honestly, she's the only woman I've met who seemed competent enough. Charlie exudes competence.

She seems to like that. She smiles, watching my face. "Your eyes almost look silver in the moonlight."

My wolf is showing? That gives me pause. I don't think that's happened before with a woman. Damn, I must really need to get laid tonight. I reach around and grasp the back of her neck, pulling her into me.

She gasps, her hands coming to my chest, her breath fogging the air between us. My mouth descends on hers in a rough kiss. A promise of what's to come.

She parts her lips, accepts my plunder. I let my tongue flick between them, a suggestion of what I'll be doing between her legs.

And then she's all in. Her arms circle around my neck and she kisses me back, abandoning whatever small resistance she still had to this. I scoop her ass up with my forearm, so she's straddling me, and carry her to her door, as our lips and tongues tangle and twist over one another.

"Here." She's breathless. She holds up her keys. I take them from her, refusing to break the kiss, and fumble with the lock without looking. It gives me the chance to press her back against the door and grind the bulge of my cock in the notch between her legs. Then the door opens and we tumble forward, laughing. I recover my balance, and my hold on her. Her scent is driving me wild now. It's up in my nostrils, creating all kinds of chaos with my wolf.

If my eyes weren't ice-blue before, they sure are now. Hopefully Charlie won't remember their color from before.

I want to carry her straight to the bedroom, but I promised her an all-nighter, and I intend to make sure she feels like breaking her own rules are worth it.

Because I'm sure this night with me is a breaking of rules. Charlie doesn't strike me as the type who picks up men at a bar. I doubt she's spontaneous or wild. Her home is clean and neat as a pin. Small, basic, but well-cared for and organized. I carry her to the dining room table—a thick, sturdy-looking slab of walnut with legs—and lay her down. She tries to remain sitting, but I push her to her back and tug off her boots.

"Um, I don't think this table will hold both of us."

I chuckle. "I'm not getting on it with you. Tables are for eating, right?"

"Oh my God," she groan-giggles, covering her face, even

though she can't know that I see her blush.

I work the button on her jeans and pull them and her panties down and off her legs while she shucks her puffy coat and jacket. "I just wanted a place to spread you out and admire you," I tell her. "Hmm." I tweak her peaked nipple through her tight t-shirt. "You are so damn cute in this t-shirt," I muse. "But no, it needs to go, too."

I strip off my leather jacket and drop it on her floor.

She helps me pull off her shirt, and I unclasp her bra and slide it down her arms as well. I grip her thighs, holding her knees up, and just stare for a moment, drinking her in. She's propped on her elbows, naked. Her breasts are a perfect handful, her frame athletic. The hair on her mons has been neatly trimmed. "Now that's a sight," I murmur.

"How can you even see me?" she asks. "The lights are off."

I nibble her inner thigh, starting at the knee and working my way up. "Did you want me to turn on the lights?" I ask between licks and nips.

"N-no." I love how breathless she sounds. "This is better."

I reach up and cup one breast, squeezing gently. I thumb over her nipple, then I reward her with my tongue, licking into her at the same time as I squeeze the peaked bud firmly.

She cries out, hips jumping, knees smacking against my shoulders. I pin her pelvis down to hold her in place as I trace inside her labia, finding the place at the apex where her tiny pleasure organ resides. I flick my tongue over it until it stiffens, and then I swirl my tongue in a circle around it. I suck one of her nether lips, releasing it with a pop.

Tremors run through Charlie. "Oh my God. Happy birthday to me."

"Yes," I rumble. "Happy birthday to you, beautiful."

CHAPTER 3

harlie

BEST. Decision. Ever.

Adele was so right. There's nothing wrong with a one-off from The Big Plan where a hot man is concerned. Especially on your birthday.

Lance hits all my buttons. Especially—*oh!*—I arch as he affixes his lips around my clit and sucks hard. Charm Boy has all the moves. Which I expected. A player's great when you're playing, right?

He's not in a hurry, but he keeps the pace elevated. I don't have time to catch my breath or adjust to the pleasure before he screws a finger inside me. He plunges it in and out a couple times, then massages my inner wall with a stroking that makes me go wild. I nearly kick him in the head, I'm so out of my mind.

"Lance," I pant.

"That's right, baby. Say my name when you feel good."

"I feel good," I admit. I have nothing to hide. I invited him in for exactly this. The least I can do is show my appreciation. "Sh-show me."

"Show you what, beautiful?" He returns his mouth to my clit, giving it a series of quick flicks that make me squeeze his finger with my muscles.

"Show me what you've got."

His laugh is deep and rumbly. "Oh, I'll show you. I'll show you all night long."

Then, to my utter shock, he flips me over and lifts my hips until I'm on my knees on the table. He spreads my cheeks, and licks from clit to anus.

"H-holy mother of God," I warble. I've never had anyone lick me that way. Or even treat me this way—like a tasty dessert he can't get enough of. And his confidence!

It's so freaking sexy.

He knows he's sex personified. He knows what he's doing and that he's damn good at it. The accountant in my plan won't be able to do this. But I'm not going to think about him right now. It's my birthday, and I'm going to enjoy every minute of it.

Lance's big hands are firm on my ass, gripping my cheeks, holding me in place as he rims my anus.

"Lance!" I'm slightly alarmed to be touched there. To be *licked* there. I mean, I showered after work, but still…

He rubs his fingers over my dripping sex, circling my clit, slipping into my entrance. His thumb presses against my asshole as two digits slide inside my pussy.

I moan wantonly. It's embarrassing but it feels so good.

"Please," I beg. I don't know what I'm begging for. Do I want him to stop? To give me more? I think I want to take this to the bedroom. "It's too much," I gasp.

He pauses, but he's not buying it. "Too much?" His

chuckle is rough. He catches me around my waist and somehow lowers me to my side, pushing the top knee wide open. "Too much what, baby? Too much pleasure?"

"Yes." I laugh, because I know that must sound ridiculous. Or maybe because I'm giddy. Possibly hysterical. I'm so close to orgasm. So close to losing my mind.

Lance returns to his self-appointed job of driving me wild with his very talented tongue. As he does, he massages my anus with his thumb, not letting me get away from that taboo pleasure. That horrible, wonderful sensation.

"No, um…"

He slides his other thumb inside me, cupping my mons as he thumb-fucks me, smacking on my clit with each in-stroke. With the other thumb, he applies pressure, and then suddenly he's breached that hole, too. Both his thumbs are inside me—double penetration! He drops a ball of his saliva to lube the way for the back hole. I'm screaming. I want it to end, but it feels so good. I'm coming apart. Totally incoherent, lost. Exploding into a million tiny pieces of myself.

I come. Both channels squeeze the hell out of his thumbs, my inner thighs shake and jerk, and I push his hips with the soles of my feet, like I want to push him away, even though he's the master of my orgasm.

"Lance."

Am I weeping? Did a rocket ship take off from my dining room? Oh God, I don't even know what just happened.

Lance eases his thumbs out and licks and kisses my lady parts some more, and then he scoops me up into his arms like I weigh nothing.

"Oh my God."

"I prefer Lance." He carries me down the hallway.

I laugh, even though he's a dork, and I bite his ear, flicking my tongue inside.

"Aw, fuck, baby. That's not playing fair."

"It's not?" I'm still so incredibly turned on. The orgasm left me weak and loose-limbed, but with a furnace of desire roaring for more.

He tries the door to my guest room. "Nope." I giggle— and I'm not the kind of girl who giggles. "Next door down."

"Why are the doors closed?" he demands as he fumbles with the handle. I reach out to help him.

"What's not fair?" I suck his earlobe into my mouth.

"I'm trying to make this about you, sweetheart. But if you keep teasing me like that, you're going to get yourself fucked hard and fast."

Another mini-orgasm ripples through me.

"Hard and fast sounds good." My voice doesn't even sound like my own, it's so husky.

Lance groans as he crawls onto my bed on his knees, still holding me in his arms. "I wanted to take my time with you."

"Oh my God, you *have*." I let my appreciation be heard in the rise of my voice. "Besides, you can always take more time after hard and fast."

He drops me on my back and does the one-handed sexy shirt removal thing that only guys can do. There's an animal-like noise coming from him. A low rumble. Almost like a growl. It's sexy as hell. His eyes almost seem to glow in the dark, the way a cat's do.

As if on cue with that thought, Merlin hisses from the direction of my desk.

"Oh, shit. I'm so sorry. Merlin's not used to me having visitors." I laugh, embarrassed. He's never done that before.

"I'll make friends with him later," Lance says, busy taking off his boots. He produces a handful of condoms from his back pocket, which he tosses on the bed.

"I guess you came prepared." I try to shove back the

misgivings I'm having about the fact that he brought so many. That he had them right in his back pocket, not tucked in a wallet. He was planning on hooking up with me.

But I knew that already, didn't I? I pick one up and open it.

"I wouldn't leave you unprotected, birthday girl."

Hmm. It sounds chivalrous, but also sounds like a line. But again, who cares? *Only one night.*

Lance has already taken off his jeans and briefs. His very hard cock springs out, impressive in its length.

"Wow."

He angles his hips like he's posing. I play along and whistle. "Very nice."

"Say hello to my wingman."

"I'm sorry, what? Did you just call your dick your wingman? Is it because he gets you laid?"

"You got it." There's that playboy smirk.

"Get over here." My girl parts are eager to get acquainted. I crook my finger at him. He crawls on the bed and positions himself between my knees. "Have you never had a woman put your condom on for you?"

"Can't say that I have," he says, sounding surprised.

"So that's two things you've let me do tonight that are firsts with women." Oh God. I don't know why I'm fishing for compliments. I guess it's some universal fantasy—wanting to be the one who reforms the rake, a fantasy which we all know never happens in real life. If the rake does settle down, he becomes a cheater. I mean, a guy who loves women that much can't go cold turkey.

Anyway. I don't need to reform Lance. It's a birthday one-night stand, and I have a plan:

1. Get this condom on
2. Ride his 'wingman' to multiple orgasms
3. Repeat until I pass out.

I'LL SLEEP WELL TONIGHT, and I won't miss him in the morning when he's gone.

I roll the condom onto his erection, loving the way it stretches even longer in my fist. "A very happy birthday to me," I murmur my approval.

"You like that? You haven't even seen what I can do with it."

I roll my eyes, which, of course, he can't see in the dim light, but there's no denying the thumping in my chest. My excitement to have him moving between my legs. I mentally thank Adele once more for encouraging me to indulge in this fling. It's already been so worth it, and we haven't even had intercourse yet.

I guide him to my entrance. I'm already more than ready, and the tip sinks in easily. Lance leans his hands on the bed above my shoulders and thrusts in, filling me. I gasp —not at the size of him, which I definitely feel, but at the rightness. It feels so good. Delicious. He eases back and pushes in again. My eyes roll back in my head with pleasure.

"Fuck, Charlie."

I'm way too satisfied to hear the playboy losing control.

I rock my hips up to meet his thrusts. He plucks one of my nipples, staring down at me with an intensity that unnerves me, all the while sliding in and out of me like it's the most important job he's ever taken.

He lowers for a kiss, but then loses concentration. His

mouth is suspended above mine, our breath mingling as he swallows my gasp.

I grip his muscled arms, leveraging my hips to snap up and meet his, trying to take him deeper, because I need more. So much more.

"Fuck," he curses again. The leash on his control snaps and then he gives what he promised—fast and hard. Turns out the placement of his hands above my shoulders was strategic, because now they act as bumpers. Each time he thrusts, I surge upward against the bracketing of his wrists.

"Yes," I gasp. It feels so good. Rough, but satisfying.

"Sorry," he pants. His eyes seem to glow. I'm not sure what he's apologizing for—maybe because he's losing control. It's not about my pleasure anymore, he's seeking his own, and yet each desperate surge inside me stokes my own fire. My desire chases the release in perfect concert with his.

"More," I gasp.

His eyes seem to glow even brighter. "Fuck." He bucks harder, slams into me. He shifts back to stand on his knees, gripping my bent legs where thigh creases into hip to yank me into him. I swear he'll split me in two. It's ravenous.

Passion like I've never known. Never seen. Never experienced for myself, because yes, I feel it too. I want him deeper. I want him to destroy me with that cock, make me forget all my worries, all my plans, everything that keeps me rigid and uptight and forgetting how to live.

"Yes!" I encourage, in case he's not sure how much I need it. "Lance… Lance."

"Baby." The word sounds broken on his lips. Like a lament. Like he can't believe how lost he is in this moment. "I can't… I need…" For a moment, I see the gleam of his canine teeth and from this angle, they seem longer and sharper than normal. He holds my hips and pummels in and out in short, quick strokes, slapping my ass with his loins, filling the room with the wanton sounds of sex.

"Ch-Charlie. Charlie." He sounds alarmed. "Oh, fuck." Lance lets out an animal-like growl as he thrusts in deep, and comes. He brings his thumb to my clit and rubs and I scream my finish, too, tightening and squeezing around his cock, my feet flying up to his shoulders.

The room spins. Or maybe the entire planet teeters. I'm not sure. I just know that I depart from the physical plane and spin off somewhere for who knows how long.

When I open my eyes again, Lance shivers and eases out. "You okay, angel?"

"Mmm. More than okay." I'm floaty, but I roll over to watch Lance. Naked Lance is a sight to behold. And his smirk tells me he knows it.

He reaches down to grip his cock, and then his eyes widen. "Oh shit. Oh, Charlie. The condom broke."

All I can do is laugh. "Well, it's no wonder. You were moving pretty fast."

I grab some tissues to clean myself up.

Lance's blue eyes lock on mine. He's probably panicking so I add, "It's okay. I'm actually on the pill."

His eyes narrow. Some strange emotion flits across his face—surprise? dismay? Whatever it is, he hides it quickly. "Great. Good. Okay."

"Don't worry." I chuckle, and pat his arm. "No harm done. I had fun."

He still doesn't look happy, but he gives a little shake of his head and lays himself out beside me, pulling me into his arms. I settle against his warm, hard body. Sex and a cuddle? This playboy is an overachiever.

"Do you cuddle all your one-night stands?" I ask. A jolt goes through him.

"No," he mutters against my neck. He still sounds upset. Poor guy, this might be his worst nightmare.

Too bad. I did have fun. And best of all, it's done, and I have no regrets. Now I can move on to dating accountants. And Lance won't care. He'll have moved on, he and his 'wingman'.

Everything is going to plan.

CHAPTER 4

L *ance*

In the morning, I get up and soundlessly dress, then go to make coffee in Charlie's kitchen. I've never stayed the night with a woman before, but last night changed everything for me.

Charlie is my mate.

I can't believe it. I never thought I'd mate. It was crazy enough that Deke of all people found his one true mate, but I didn't expect it for the rest of us. It's unusual to find one's true mate, for one thing. Of all the shifters on the planet, you have to get the scent of the one that's for you. And Charlie's not even a shifter!

Now I understand why her scent was so tantalizing down at the hot springs.

Now I know why I couldn't let the thought of her go yesterday. Why I had to spend all afternoon cyber-stalking her, and then all evening *literally* stalking her just to get her in bed.

Only my wolf doesn't just want her in bed.

He wants her forever.

That sex last night wasn't just sex. I lost control unexpectedly because he wanted me to mark her, right there. It's no wonder I pounded her so hard, the condom got lost.

Fuck, I hope I didn't leave her too sore. I don't know—I might have even used shifter strength on her. I totally lost my mind for a few moments there.

And now that I know Charlie's mine… Now that I've tasted her, been inside her, I almost wish I hadn't. Not because I don't intend to claim her—I do.

But I wish I could have a do-over.

Because I'm not sure Charlie even really likes me. She has this idea I'm a player. Which I suppose I am.

Was.

Charlie wanted me last night—no doubt about that—but she definitely gave the impression that this was a one-night-stand. A fling. Just for fun. The result of me showing up at the perfect time on her birthday night. I mean, that was what I was going for. What I offered.

She's probably going to be surprised to discover I'm still here, waiting in her kitchen for her to wake up and smell the coffee I'm making.

My leg jiggles up and down like I'm a horny, restless teen shifter. I've been like this since last night. I didn't sleep more than half an hour. The rest of the time I spent staring at my beautiful female, which I'm sure she would've found a bit creepy if she'd woken.

Finally, I hear movement from the bedroom. The toilet flushes. An electric toothbrush runs. Charlie pads out to the kitchen in her bare feet, wearing one of her sassy t-shirts and a pair of hot pink panties.

I have to swallow the possessive growl that rises up in my throat.

Fuck.

I'm going to have to really keep my wolf in check if I have any hope of getting a second date with her. She probably wouldn't take kindly to: *you're mine and I must possess and protect you for the rest of my life or I'll turn into a feral beast that needs to be put down.*

Sure enough, she gives me a strange look. "You made coffee, huh?"

I shrug, trying very hard to appear casual as I pour her a mug. "I figured I should ride you back to your car before work."

"Good point." She blushes, like she's regretting last night. *Damn.*

"Great. Yeah, thanks. That's a good idea." She hides her face in the coffee cup, taking a long sip. "So I will just, um, get showered." She gives me an up and down sweep of her eyes. Either she's remembering what it felt like to have this body over hers last night, or she wants more.

"Need any help?" It sounds as lame to my ears as I feared it would. What's wrong with me? Have I suddenly lost all game with women?

But Charlie's not a game.

I don't want to use charm and coax another interlude out of her. I want real connection. I need her to want more than one night.

"Um, no, I'm good." She says it way too fast.

Crushingly fast.

I really couldn't have fucked this up more.

She turns on her cute little barefooted heel and disappears to the bathroom, and I'm left with a jumbo-sized boner that is likely to kill me. I'll be jerking in my shower the second I get home.

Speaking of home, I'm going to have to explain my absence last night to Rafe. Of course, he'll assume I'm being my usual, careless womanizing self, and breaking the rules to dip my stick in another human.

He'll give me shit but it won't be anything he doesn't expect from me.

The question is, do I tell him about Charlie? Not that I fucked her, but that she's my mate?

No. It feels too private, and far too tenuous. I mean, I don't even know if I'm going to get a second date with this female, and landing it feels like a national fucking emergency. I'm too tender to absorb Rafe's disapproval, or a repetition of his rules about who I can and can't fuck.

A black cat yarls at me and jumps onto the counter, tail puffy, ears back. He smells danger.

"Oh, right. You must be Merlin." I pick him up by the nape and hold him up at eye-level, giving a low warning growl to show him what I am, and who's alpha here.

The moment I set him back on his feet, he drops to his side and shows his belly in submission in a decidedly dog-like manner.

"Smart kitty." I stroke his soft cheeks to reward him. He takes it for a few moments, then springs back up and trots away, apparently cool with me now.

I listen to the sound of the shower turn off, and have to work hard not to picture Charlie coming out of her bathroom, dripping and naked, that glorious body begging to be taken again.

No. I doubt she wants round two right now.

In fact, my gut says she doesn't want another round at all, so I need to get my mind off fucking her and start figuring out how to get her on a date. I walk around her place, memorizing every detail. There's a photo on her refrigerator of a young man in uniform—must be the brother. Another one of her whole family—the parents, Charlie, and her brother. A few coupons are stuck under magnets, and a card for a plumber and one for the chimney sweep.

I take in Charlie's furniture, sparing a moment to savor the memory of Charlie served up on the dining table for me. Like the table, all her furniture is sturdy and practical. Well-made. Not expensive, but not cheap, throwaway crap either. She has a red Turkish rug in the living room, and a brown leather couch and chair set oriented to face either the kiva fireplace or the television.

The interior paint is a pale mustard, except for an accent wall of brick red. The house is southwestern without beating you over the head with it. There's no coyote with a handkerchief or horned skull on the mantle, but there is a mirror framed with cheerful Mexican tile, and another colorful piece of art.

Charlie emerges in her work uniform, which shouldn't look hot. I mean, the U.S. Postal Service wasn't going for sexy when they designed the blue uniforms, but for some reason, I sprout a semi from the way the fabric drapes across her perfect tits. The flash of skin at her throat. Her pine and peach scent that fills my nostrils.

I clear my throat, turning away so she won't see how excited I am to see her.

I rinse my coffee mug out in the sink and put it in the dishwasher.

"Thanks." Charlie eyes me like she's surprised I'm house trained enough to put away my own dishes.

"You ready? I mean, there's no rush."

"No, I'm ready." She grabs her puffy coat from the hook by the door and then hands me my leather one. I hung it there this morning when I got up and found it on the floor under the table.

I slip it on. "You want to drive?"

She shakes her head.

The fun is over. Whatever willingness Charlie had last night to explore and play with me, it's gone. It's no longer her birthday. The permission she gave herself to indulge has passed.

I try not to let the low grumble of my wolf come out of my throat. It's no problem.

I'll get the second date.

I just may have to work a lot harder for it than I did for the first one.

~

Charlie

There's nothing worse than the morning after a one-night stand. I mean, it's not really supposed to happen, right? The morning-after part? The person who slept over is supposed to sneak out at dawn before the other one is awake. Or, at worst, make a mad scramble to grab their clothes and jet the moment they realize where they are.

It's not a stay and make coffee kind of scenario.

And riding on the back of Lance's Duck or Duke or whatever he calls it to Arroyo Seco just to get my car to drive back into town to work feels all wrong.

Irresponsible. Foolish. Definitely shameful.

I'm literally doing the ride of shame right now. I let the player get in my pants last night and now the whole town will know.

Not that the people of Taos give two fucks about who I screw. It's a small town, but it's not that kind of small town. Maybe if I we were both born and raised here, someone might take note, but no one's taking notes on my sex life except me.

And maybe Adele, who sent me a text last night saying: *Screw the plan.*

Well, I screwed something. He definitely wasn't the plan, though.

The thought of all that screwing makes me rock my hips down over the vibrating seat. My hands rest lightly on Lance's hips. It feels precarious, but I didn't want to make direct contact with those washboard abs by holding onto his waist. I tuck a finger through his belt loop, as if that will hold me in place if we get thrown.

Because in the light of day, the Ducati seems like an extremely dangerous machine. Like, where are the seatbelts? And what the hell was I thinking actually driving this thing last night? And for all its speed and power, it's no comparison to the man driving it. He's truly a specimen of the ultimate in masculinity. Hard-bodied. Smooth-talking. Sex on wheels.

But there's no danger today of me falling into bed with him again.

He was good. Extremely talented at making me come, but definitely not my type. No need to go down that path again.

He pulls into the parking lot of the restaurant where my Subaru is still parked, and stops beside it.

I unbuckle his helmet and climb off, then hand it to him. "Thanks for the ride. And for last night."

"Definitely my pleasure." He leans on one foot, balancing the bike beneath those powerful thighs. I try to ignore how good he looks in the leather jacket and the motorcycle underneath him. A bad boy out on the prowl. "You want to get dinner sometime?"

Huh. I didn't expect him to ask me out. But then, I hadn't expected him to make coffee, either. It's a little weird. Lance didn't strike me as the clingy type last night. Far from it.

"Um, no, I'm good." I put an apology into my expression.

"Let me guess—you don't date military guys?"

I blink in surprise, then laugh, disarmed. This guy wrote the manual on charm. That cock-sure teasing way he has of getting right to the point probably gets him right into the panties of every girl he turns it on.

"Actually, I do have a rule against it. No offense to you. Last night was really fun. It was just... not something I usually do."

"Yeah, I get it. Birthday fucks are fun." He still doesn't leave. "I guess this is where I refrain from asking for your number."

"Um, yeah. Sorry."

I can't blame a guy for trying. I mean, I expected him to get my number for another booty call. It was the dinner date part that surprised me.

"Well, I like you, Charlie. I want to see you again—with your clothes on. So if you change your mind, let me know." He hands me a card.

"Uh... okay. Thanks." I wave the card lamely, then back up and turn to open my car door.

"I mean, clothes off is cool, too," Lance says to my back.

I turn, shaking my head, a reluctant smile twisting on my lips. There's that playboy.

"I'm down with seeing you in any state of dress or undress."

"I'm sure you are." I toss him a smile as I climb into my car. "I'll see you around."

His smile dips a fraction. I'm sure he's not used to striking out. He puts the helmet on, watching me as I start the car and pull out.

As I drive back into town, I shake my head, confused. It was weird that he tried for a second date. Players don't usually try to hit it again so soon.

But I don't need to give last night so much mental real estate. It was a one-off. For fun. For my birthday.

It won't be happening again. I didn't agree to see Lance again. I won't be calling him for that date, or for a booty call or any other reason.

I have a plan, and I'm sticking to it.

CHAPTER 5

$\mathcal{L}$ *ance*

"MOVE IT."

"What's gotten into you?" Channing asks as I elbow him out of the way of the refrigerator. The guy seems to have taken up permanent residence standing in the open door, staring at the food.

I reach past him and grab three packages of bacon, not bothering to answer.

I admit I've been cranky as hell lately. The wound of being shot down by Charlie for a second date has festered all week. I rejected my frequently recurring idea to go and arrange a 'chance' meeting with her in town. Charlie is smart —she wouldn't buy it, and I don't want to come off as desperate.

Which I am, by the way.

This woman is under my skin in a big, bad way. An I-can't-sleep-at-night-because-I'm-thinking-of-her way. And jerking off five times a day does nothing to relieve the mounting pressure to get inside her again.

I couldn't have fucked this one up more. I tear open the packages of bacon with my teeth and throw the contents of all three into a cast iron pan.

"Seriously, dude. You've been an asshole all week. Ever since—" He stops with a look of surprise on his face, like he thinks he's put something together. "Ah…"

I want to kill the guy.

"Ever since what?" Rafe asks.

Fuck. Now I'm really going to kill Channing.

"Who did you say you spent the night with last week?" Channing asks.

Rafe folds his arms over his chest, leaning one shoulder in the doorframe of the kitchen of our old ski lodge turned headquarters. "I don't think you did say, did you?" He tips his head, his sharp alpha gaze suddenly trained on my face.

"Fuck you both." Gah. Now I've basically acknowledged that Charlie is the cause of my distemper.

"I don't believe it. Did Fate kick you in the nuts, Lance?" Channing chortles.

Rafe stiffens, even though his posture doesn't change.

I rub the back of my neck. Rafe is going to flip, but if Charlie really is my mate, and the fact that I sprouted fangs and wanted to mark her that night proves she is, then this shit is going to come out anyway.

My pack will have to hold my collar if I go off the deep end.

So I don't attempt to lie. Instead, I say, "I don't want to talk about it."

"Oh, we're talking about it." Rafe is suddenly in motion, crossing the kitchen to pen me in against the stove.

Channing follows his alpha, and takes up my other side.

I don't mean to, but a growl comes out of my throat, as if the two of them are trying to keep me from my mate.

"Did you just fucking growl at me?" Rafe demands. He's not just my big brother, he's pack alpha, meaning his dominance rules here.

"Who is it?" Channing wants to know.

"A friend of Sadie's," I admit.

"*Which friend?*" The ferocity in Rafe's voice makes me wonder if his interest in Adele, the prickly chocolatier, isn't also fate-related. But Rafe would never mate.

"Charlie. The blonde. We hooked up; that's it. She's not interested in seeing me again."

Rafe's gaze narrows. "But you're interested?"

There's no point in lying. Rafe would smell it anyway.

"My wolf came out," I admit. "He wanted to claim her."

Rafe takes a step back and shakes his head. "Fuck."

"I'm sorry. I never intended to mate. I definitely wasn't looking. I mean, she's a human!"

"Fate kicked you in the nuts." Channing is so fucking thrilled with himself for figuring it out.

"Shut up, asshole."

"What are you going to do?" Rafe asks. There's warning in his tone. A hint of danger.

I shrug. "What can I do? I have to convince her to see me again. Every day that goes on... gets harder."

"Son of a bitch." Rafe turns away.

"Tell me about it."

"The player got played." Channing's still way too gleeful about my sitch.

"Played by Charlie?" I snarl.

His perfect toothpaste-commercial smile widens even more. "Played by Fate, sucka."

"I really don't know why you find this so amusing."

"Neither do I." Rafe backs me up, for once, sending Channing a quelling look. To me, he says, "You're sure? She's yours?"

"I'm hers," I say miserably. I don't dare tell my alpha that I've reduced myself to stalking her in wolf form along her mail route every day just to stay near her. Just because the need to protect her, to keep other males away from her, is so strong, it consumes me.

Rafe's brows pop. "Well. I guess you'd better figure out how to get that second date." He says it like it's a military order.

I rub my hand over my short hair. "Yes, sir."

I flip the sizzling bacon and tear open a five pound package of ground beef to go with it. I need all the fuel I can get. This need to mate Charlie is running me dry.

After I make a dozen hamburgers piled high with bacon, I take them out to my workstation. I've been working on the only angle I could come up with for Charlie: her brother Chad. Charlie's worried about him because he's been out of contact. That happens in the military, especially when soldiers are on a tour. It doesn't mean he's necessarily in any more danger than usual.

I call Colonel Johnson. He's the officer who put together our Shifter Forces team. A lion himself, he literally sniffed out shifters in the service and invited them to serve on elite nightwalker teams. He put our shifter skills—night vision, strength, speed, spontaneous healing—to good use, and by putting us only with our own kind, he ensured we didn't have to hide what we were.

Not all Shifter Forces teams are grouped by species, but we wolves were, because we already function well as a pack. We follow our alpha implicitly. Of course, it also means our pack would follow an order from Rafe over an order from the colonel, but that was a chance Colonel Johnson was willing to take.

Colonel Johnson answers on the second ring. "Corporal, I located your fly-boy."

"Great."

"He's flying combat in Syria—active air strikes."

I curse inwardly. "I've got a favor to ask—it's pretty big."

"I can't pull that kid out of there," Colonel Johnson says immediately.

"Not that big."

"What do you need?"

"Any chance I could get five minutes of video conferencing with him?"

"What's this about?" the colonel demands.

"It's about a female, Colonel," I snap back, my patience a frayed wire.

"I don't follow."

"He's my mate's brother. She's worried about him. I'd just like to give her a chance to connect with him. Can you hook me up?"

Colonel Johnson lets out a low chuckle. "Fate caught up to you, did she? Lotta women gonna mourn the loss of you on the playing field."

"Well, it's not in the bag yet, so I'd appreciate this solid."

"Oh. You haven't claimed her yet? And she's human? That doesn't bode well."

I bite back the *fuck you* that rises to my lips. "No, sir."

"Okay, Corporal. I'll see what I can do."

"I owe you. Big time."

"Don't thank me yet. I just said I'd see."

"I appreciate it, Colonel."

I hang up and bring my empty plate to the kitchen,

thinking of Charlie when I put it in the dishwasher. Everything makes me think of Charlie.

She'll be out on her route right now.

Which means… that's where I need to be, too.

I slip out the door and climb on my bike to ride it down the mountain. Once I get close to town, I hide the bike, strip off my clothes, and shift.

~

Charlie

I get out of the mail truck and tuck the mail into the boxes on the bank of mailboxes at the corner, then sling my bag over my shoulder to walk along the dirt road and deliver the rest.

I'm nerved up because I've been seeing a wolf on my mail route lately. It's big and grey with a splash of white on its nose. And it's fucking huge. Wolves look so cute in the Save the Planet calendars I get in the mail—the ones with beautiful wildlife photos of coral reefs and baby elephants. I'm a sucker for donating to Save the Planet type causes, so I get tons of these types of calendars free. There's always a cute and fluffy wolf featured in one or two of the months.

In real life, wolves are not fluffy. They are not cute. They are massive, graceful, super deadly predators, and the sight of them activates the *OH SHIT* part of your brain. The part that tells you to *Run!*

Except all I do is freeze mid-step, with my mailbag heavy on my hip.

I've seen the wolf three times this week, which is downright weird, considering they have a huge territory.

I'm three quarters of the way down the road when I spot him. I freeze, careful not to make eye contact.

52

"Nice wolfie," I call nervously. My mail person training never covered what to do when confronted with endangered wildlife. Aggressive dogs, yes. Attack squirrels, yes (don't ask). Disgruntled people. Rain, sleet, and snow.

But not big-ass wolves with *my, what big teeth you have* muzzles and yellow eyes.

Fuck fuck fuck. What do I do?

Whelp, you're gonna die, my frontal lobe offers helpfully.

I review my options:

1. Pee myself
2. Run away and hope the wolf doesn't chase me. Too much to hope I can outrun it
3. Fall down and play dead

I think option number one is a certainty no matter what I choose.

I go with a fourth option. "Nice wolfie. Good wolfie." I sidle away.

He keeps his distance, trotting along beside me, but a good fifty feet away. He doesn't seem to be hunting me. I mean, he'd square off to me if he were, right?

"Nice wolfie," I say again, darting another glance at him. He stops and sits with a little whine.

Huh?

Could he be someone's domesticated wolf-dog?

But no way. I mean, this wolf is huge.

I'm so busy worrying about the wolf, I forget to worry about my feet, and trip over a loose stone.

Eek!

I go down, flat on my face, belly, and hands. The mailbag spills its contents, but that's not the part that freaks me out. It's the wolf sprinting for me.

"No!" I shriek, scrambling to my feet. The last thing I need to do is lie on the ground and offer my neck like a sacrificial goat. Or lamb. Whatever.

Amazingly, the wolf skids to a stop, leaving twenty feet between us. He lowers his head, almost like an apology, then turns and trots away, glancing over his shoulder a couple times. What the F? Seriously—what is up with that crazy wolf? When he disappears behind the sagebrush, I let out a long, shaky breath and bend my trembling legs to start picking up the mail scattered across the dirt.

Now, belatedly, I remember I have pepper spray clipped to my bag. Lot of good it did me there. Well, if it happens again, I'll be prepared.

∼

Lance

I pull up in front of Charlie's house at 9:00 p.m. I'm itchy and edgy. I feel like I need to shift and run off the excess energy, but I just did that. Literally. I ran all evening, then showered and changed to come here.

I'm still wincing over seeing Charlie fall on her face today. I'm the biggest asshole. I didn't mean to scare her, but of course I did. My wolf is huge, and she felt threatened. The reminder that she's human—fragile and breakable and completely in the dark about my kind—hit me hard.

It had me questioning whether I was wrong about her being my mate. I mean, why would Fate choose a human for me? I'm not alpha of my pack, but I could be. I'd certainly be at the head of any pack. Pairing an alpha male with a human doesn't make sense. Not when our species is already dwindling.

Standing in front of her door, though, all my doubt

vanishes. Her scent lingers everywhere, prickling at my skin, sending my blood south. Her effect on me is undeniable.

I'm ready to beat down her door to get to her, then throw her over my shoulder and carry her home, caveman style.

Too bad that won't fly. I raise my fist to knock. She's going to think this is a booty-call visit. Showing up at nine at night? This isn't going to look good.

If she'd given me her number, I could've texted her before I came over. Of course, I have access to her number. I looked it up and put it in my phone the minute I got home the morning after her birthday. But I figured texting without her permission wasn't going to fly any better than showing up, so here I am.

I rap on the door with my knuckles, shifting on my feet.

Fates, I've never been so nervous with a female before. I was the kid who had girlfriends by age ten. I literally was *born* with game. Rafe got the serious gene. I got the player one.

Nah, that's not true. We weren't born to these roles. Rafe wasn't born with a stick up his ass. He was a normal shifter kid before our parents' murder. But the PTSD of that trauma forced him into the role of alpha far too early, and he took the whole world on his shoulders. He refused to let me take any responsibility at all, other than to do what he said. So I guess I purposely took on the role of playboy. It was that, or resent the hell out of Rafe for treating me like a fucking baby.

I hear Charlie moving inside. She looks through the peephole at me.

I hold up my palms. "It's not a booty call. I have a surprise for you." My breath catches and holds as she remains still for a moment inside. When she opens the door, my heart starts beating again.

"May I come in? I promise you're going to like it."

Charlie's in a tit-hugging threadbare graphic tee with no bra, and a pair of loose pajama bottoms that fall below her hips, giving me a view of a swath of bare skin at her midriff that makes my mouth water. She folds her arms across her apple-sized breasts and cocks a hip. "What is it?"

"Please don't make me spoil the surprise. I swear on everything holy you will be glad you let me in." Yeah, I'm literally reduced to begging here. My female has zero interest in me. How can this be?

Except, that's not true. Because I see her nipples—hard and stiff—poking out through that shirt behind her crossed arms. That confidence boost is all I need to turn on the charm. I lean one hand against her house, giving her my best pirate smile.

She leans in toward me. I don't even think she means to, but it's like my body calls to hers. Her face gets closer to mine and I breathe in her pine and peaches scent. My semi grows. My wolf is both appeased and incensed at being so close to her. My heartbeat picks up. I risk a casual touch, brushing a lock of pale hair from her eyes.

"Come on, don't leave me hanging out here."

Charlie's smile is reluctant. She grabs a fistful of my leather jacket and tugs me inside, walking backward in the cutest possible way. I know, backward walking isn't meant to be cute, but fuck—on this woman—it's insanely adorable. I check out her bare feet. Her toes are polished in bubblegum pink and I make a mental note to suck every single one of them as soon as possible.

I pretend to mop my brow. "Whew. You had me sweating it for a minute there, and we don't have much time. Come on." I take her hand and tug her to the couch, where I sit down. When she hesitates, I reach for her waist and pull her onto my lap.

"Oh!" she exclaims, one of her cute bare feet kicking out.

"See what happens when you don't trust?"

The scent of her arousal blooms as she squirms on my knee, catching hold of my shoulders to steady herself.

I'm dying to explore this position way more intimately, but there's no time. Besides, I'm supposed to be proving I'm *not* here for a booty call.

I turn on my phone and flick open the email from Colonel Johnson, then click the link he sent me.

"What is this?"

"Just wait, angel. It's coming." The spinner spins on my screen as the teleconference loads. Then it brings up an empty screen.

Charlie looks at me. "I really don't under—"

An image appears. A handsome but tired-looking young man in uniform blinks at the screen. "Charlie?"

"Oh my God, Chad!" Charlie covers her mouth with her hand, snatching the phone from my hand and surging up from my lap. She spins to give me exaggerated bug-eyes.

"Is everything okay? What's going on?" Chad sounds alarmed.

"Yes! Everything's okay! I don't even know what's going on. I was worried about you and..." —she shoots an apologetic glance my way— "I guess my friend arranged this for me." She mouths the words, *thank you* at me.

I'll be following up for more of her thanks later.

All fucking night.

No—no. That's wrong. I'm not here to get my dick wet. I'm here to *court* Charlie. As if I have any clue what that means or how to do it. If she were a wolf, it would be so easy. One sniff and she would know she belonged to me. She might kick up a little fuss at being claimed—make me work for it a little, but there'd be no question that I would prevail.

But with a human female—fuck.

I don't even know how to begin explaining to Charlie what she means to me. How I'm biologically *required* to mate with her, whether she likes it or not. I mean, of course, I'd *make* her like it. I'd devote my fucking life to ensuring my female was satisfied on every level.

But I don't know how to smooth my way into this. Getting from Point A, post one-night-stand to Point B, claiming her as my lifelong mate, feels pretty damn daunting at the moment.

But at least I got this right. Charlie's face is bright with emotion as she questions her brother.

"I can't tell you that, either, sis," Chad says when she asks where he is. "Everything's classified, that's why I haven't been in touch. And Sarge says I only have two more minutes before they have to end this call, but I'm so glad I got to tell you happy birthday to your face."

"Yeah, me too. Seeing you is the best birthday present ever." Her warm gaze flicks to me, making my dick go rock hard.

"So who was it who set this up?" Chad asks.

Charlie blushes. "Um, this guy. My friend." She sends me another look, this time with curiosity ablaze. "I don't even know how he set it up. He's former Special Forces."

"Mmm, he's got the inside hookup. Sounds like a bigshot. What kind of friend is this?"

Charlie turns her back on me. "None of your business," she says tartly.

"Oh, so it's like that?" Her brother chuckles.

"Time's up," a gruff voice barks.

"Sorry, sis, I gotta go. Tell Mom and Dad I love them. And you, too."

"I love you, too. Take care of yourself, Chad."

"Yep, I will. Bye."

Charlie keeps her back to me for a moment and I rub the back of my neck, wondering if I should leave. When she turns, her eyes are bright with tears. "Thank you," she says.

"Told ya you wouldn't be sorry."

She shakes her head. "Not sorry. That was really, really nice of you."

I get up from the couch, because it's not looking like she's going to sit back down with me. I step into her space, slowly. Close enough to be suggestive, far enough away to stay respectful. I reach out and lightly rest my hand on the curve of her hip, savoring the feel of that band of bare skin under my palm. "You're welcome."

"How did you do it? You really are that well connected?"

I shrug. "Getting a five minute call wasn't that hard. Getting him out of there would be."

Her face clouds and I kick myself for ruining the mood, but it's not fair not to be honest with her.

"So he is in a dangerous zone? I mean, I figured he must be if he couldn't tell me anything."

"I can't tell you either, but yeah. He's in the thick of it right now."

Her face falls. "I knew it had to be something like that."

I want to tell her something like, *He'll be all right*, but the truth is, I don't know. He's human, like she is. Their lives are so fragile. "I'm sorry, angel. I'll keep close tabs on his unit, okay?"

She studies my face, then blurts, "Why?"

I falter. Playboy Lance knows exactly how to play this. How to turn this into a sex-charged conversation that leads to the bedroom and me getting into those sexy pajama pants. But another one-night stand isn't my objective.

"I told you—I like you, Charlie." I take my phone from

her hand and tuck it in my back pocket, then I step in close to touch her waist again. I lower my face, hovering an inch above hers. Our gazes lock. Her breath catches and stops.

I slide my hand behind her head to cradle it.

"Fuck it," Charlie says, grasping the lapels of my jacket and lifting onto her toes to kiss me.

For one glorious moment, I kiss her back, my mouth descending over hers, drinking from her lips. My tongue slides into her mouth with a slow, sensuous pulse. It's not a practiced kiss. I forget all finesse. It's not the dominant, claiming one my wolf wants me to lay on her, either. No, I'm fully present. I'm following the moment, tasting her, following her beautiful lead. Seeing where it takes us. Her soft breasts brush against my chest, her scent gets up in my nose.

And then the *fuck it* registers.

I ease back. "Hang on a sec, angel. What does *fuck it* mean?"

Charlie's pupils are blown, her cheeks flushed. She rubs her swollen lips together. "I mean... one more round can't hurt, right?" she says.

Fuck.

I force myself to put a little space between us so I can breathe. So I can think.

"Come on, angel. I know I'm easy, but I'm angling for dinner first this time."

Some of the focus comes back to her eyes. "What?" Those sweet nipples are giving me a full salute through her thin blue t-shirt with a faded rainbow across her tits. I can't resist reaching out to lightly brush one with the pad of my thumb.

I'm rewarded with the scent of her arousal.

I slap her with my most charming smile. "You heard me."

"Lance…" I can read her indecision. She doesn't want to, but thinks she probably owes me now. I know I'm a jackass for leveraging her into this, but I can't bring myself to let her off the hook. If I give in and have sex with her tonight, I stand the chance of her writing me off as just a good fuck.

I want—*need*—so much more than that. Fuck, I need everything from her. Her entire life, future, existence.

It's either that, or I face death.

"I guess I owe you," she says.

My smile widens. My fingertips lightly mold around the side of her ribs where my thumb can still reach her nipple. I don't touch it again, though. It just hovers, ready to strike. "You do."

She looks down at my poised thumb. "So you're just going to rile me up and leave, then?"

"Kind of a dick move, isn't it?"

That elicits a throaty laugh from her. "Kind of."

"I'll tell you what. I'll stay and give you what you need, if you promise I still get dinner."

Her hesitation costs me oceans of self-respect. To make matters worse, if she turns me down, I'm sure I'll die of blue balls. So I do what I'm good at, stepping into her space and touching her waist. I slide both palms up the inside of her t-shirt along her ribs, and thumb both nipples from the inside. I keep my touch light—just a brushing tease, enough to drive her mad and make her chase it.

It works.

"Fine," she says, reaching for my jacket and shoving it down my arms. I let it drop to the floor, and tug my shirt off using one hand below my nape.

Charlie's hands are already coasting up my abs. The suddenness of her acquiescence makes me lose all game. I'm rougher than I mean to be when I take a fistful of her hair to bring her face to mine. My kiss is an assault—bruising, claiming. So fucking needy. I suck her tongue, bite her lips. She scratches my shoulders, her legs trying to climb me.

I force her backward swiftly until she hits the wall and then my hand dives into her pajama pants to palm her sweet pussy. She's not wearing panties, and she's dripping wet for me.

"Lance."

I fucking love the breathless utterance.

"It's me, baby. Keep saying my name."

"You are so cheesy," she complains, but her voice is far too husky for me to take it as an insult.

"You want me to shut up?" I screw one finger into her as my open mouth drags along her jaw. I bite her ear.

She whimpers, her internal walls clenching around my finger. "I-I didn't say that."

I ease my finger out, then fuck her with two. My palm presses against her clit as I sweep my fingers along her inside wall. "Do you like dirty talk, Charlie?" I ease both fingers out and yank down her pajama pants, dropping to a crouch in front of her.

"Um…"

"Take your shirt off." I tinge my voice with alpha command. Not on purpose—she's not a wolf—it just came out like that. I lift one of her knees and toss it over my biceps to get access to her pussy.

She obeys immediately, even though I wouldn't say my female is the obedient type. Maybe alpha command works a little on humans, too. Or maybe she just likes a take-charge guy. All that resistance is because she's afraid what would happen if she let go. Let someone else drive. She needs to stay in control to think she's safe.

I'm gonna show her there's something else. So much more.

"Hold your breasts." I lick into her and she shrieks at the contact. Her hands fall to my shoulders. I remove my tongue and pin her with a stern look. "Hands on your breasts."

She sucks in a sharp breath as if she really did feel my alpha command viscerally, the way we do. Her hands jump to cup her breasts.

I hold her gaze. "Play with them." I wait until she starts to squeeze her breasts, her belly shuddering in on a breath before I slide my tongue between her nether lips again.

"Ahh... uhn."

Her cries are delicious. So is the tangy taste of her. I trace around her inner lips, then penetrate her with my tongue, pinning her hips against the wall with one hand, the other braced against the wall to hold her knee up. I lick up and down her slit, swirling around her clit. I start to lose my mind with the scent of her and I lick and suck faster, more furiously.

"Oh... oh, *Lance!*" Her hands grasp my shoulders again.

I lift my head. "Uh-oh." I catch her wrists. "I told you where I wanted these."

Her green eyes widen in surprise. I tug her down to the floor, catching her around the waist to guide her fall. I spin her and place her on her knees.

"Now you're in trouble." There's laughter in my voice. I give her ass a light slap.

She gasps and looks over her shoulder. Her eyes are dark and there's a wild, feral quality to her I haven't seen before.

"You like that?"

"I-I don't know."

I spank her again, a little more firmly. "I'm pretty sure

you do." Honey drips from her slit. I slide a finger through her juices. She moans.

"Down on your forearms, beautiful."

When she doesn't move, I give her a sharp spank that makes her squeal. "Oh my God. You're... crazy."

"You love it." I press between her shoulder blades to encourage her down to the carpet. She follows my guidance. "That's it, angel. Now tell me how you wanna get fucked." I open my jeans to free my straining cock.

"You're so... dirty."

"Mm hm. You didn't answer me when I asked if you liked it." I sheath my cock with a condom, and drag the head along her slit.

"I like it," she admits. My wolf does a victory flip.

"Good." I grip her hip with one hand and press in. She pushes back on me and I slide in deep.

She groans.

"You feel so good, Charlie."

"Oh my God."

I fill her and retreat, savoring the way her slick walls squeeze my cock tight. It occurs to me that this was exactly the scene I'd meant to avoid. Giving Charlie rug burns while I nailed her from behind on her living room floor wasn't the get-to-know-me kind of date I had in mind. But now that we're here, I'm helpless to stop myself. I need to hear her scream. Need her to come all over my cock like I need my next breath. Satisfying my female is a drive that will never go away. Not that I'd want it to.

"Yes," Charlie breathes.

"That feel good, angel?" I can't help it. I start pumping faster.

"Y-yes. So good."

Damn. I'm lost. I slap into her forcefully, gripping her hips to hold her in place.

"Oh, yes!" She sounds surprised. Alarmed.

"You gonna come all over my cock, Charlie? Squeeze it tight when you go off like a rocket?"

She whimpers.

"Reach under and rub your clit," I tell her, because apparently I'm Mr. Bossy when it comes to making Charlie come.

She reaches between her legs, her fingers brushing the base of my cock, the place where we're joined together. Instead of rubbing her own clit, she scissors her fingers around the base of my cock, giving me the extra sensation of her fingers there.

"Fuck!" I curse because I'm getting damn close. I barely lasted fifteen minutes, and my female hasn't even come yet.

I reach out and grab a fistful of her short hair, tugging her head back. "Come for me, Charlie. Come all over my cock."

Her lithe back arches to accommodate the position I'm holding her in. She cries out in protest, but miraculously, it works. Her muscles pulse and squeeze. I stay deep inside and hold her head captive until she finishes, and the moment she does, I pull out.

"Come here, angel. I don't want to bruise your knees." I wrap my arm around her waist and help her to stand. Keeping my arm firmly around her, I walk her forward to the sofa and fold her over the stuffed arm.

"Spread those legs for me."

I push her ass cheeks wide before she complies, drinking in the sight of her most intimate parts. Her tight little rosebud anus and that swollen, dripping pussy. "So beautiful," I mutter.

She slides her legs wider, twisting her head to look in my

direction. There's an element of shock in her expression. No one's ever given it to her dirty or rough before.

I shouldn't be proud of myself for going there, but I can tell how much she loves it, even though it's out of her comfort zone.

I prod her back entrance with my cock just to tease her.

She gasps, reaching back with one hand, kicking one leg.

"Too soon?" I joke. I press back into her pussy. "I'm gonna take that ass next time, and you're going to like it."

"There is no next time," she tells me, breaking my fucking heart.

I soldier on, though. "We have a date," I remind her. I force myself to arc in and out of her slowly.

"A *dinner* date." She'd be more believable if she wasn't so breathless. If her throat didn't sound hoarse from crying out while I fucked her.

"We'll see," I say, even though sex after the date isn't my end goal. My end goal is getting another date. And another one. Convincing my beautiful female she can't live without me.

I work my hand under her hips to find her clit. "How do you like to touch yourself, Charlie?" I rub the little nubbin with the pad of my finger.

"Oh! Yes."

"Like this? Or is it more... this way?" I slow down and rub in a little circle.

"Lance," she pants.

"Uh-huh," I purr. *Say my name, beautiful.*

"I need more."

"More here?" I circle some more. "Or more here?" I shove in with a deep thrust.

"There. I need you. Harder." She sounds desperate even though she already came.

"Aw, baby. I'll give you everything you need. I promise."
I lean one hand against the sofa and pound into her, my vision
swimming as pleasure overtakes me. But I remember hers. I
tap-tap-tap over her clit, then rub.

"Yes, *yes!*" she screams.

I let out distinctly wolf-like snarl right before I come like
a fucking freight train. Her muscles squeeze as she comes in
perfect timing with me. I move my hand out from under her
hips and stroke my palm down her slender, bare back. Beautiful, beautiful human.

~

Charlie

Whoa.

Just wow. It's really hard to imagine how any guy could
top sex with Lance. I mean, our chemistry is off the charts.
Or, wait. Is it just because his experience level is off the
charts?

I need to remember that this guy is a player. He is not the
stable, secure man I'm looking to settle down with. I want a
kinder, gentler man who will be safe and stick for good.
Someone like a schoolteacher. A sweet veterinarian. A
dentist, even.

My body apparently doesn't care about my mental rejec-
tion of Lance, though. It hums and purrs with pleasure. You'd
think a player like Lance would make me feel out of my
depth sex-wise. But it's the opposite. I've never felt sexier.
Hotter. He pulls out that bossy tone with me, and I turn to
butter.

Yum.

It's so wrong that I want to do this again with him. Soon.
Very, very wrong.

Lance wraps an arm under my breasts to lift me upright before he eases out, then leaves me to take care of the condom in the bathroom wastebasket. I manage to stand on my wobbly legs enough to pick up my pajamas and slip them back on as he returns.

"Give me your number, angel." There's that bossy tone again. He's cocky as hell. I would find it annoying except for the fact that he also manages to pay attention to me. Something I never expected from a guy like him.

I mean, tracking down my brother?

That was freaking *epic.*

I definitely owe him. It's funny how he made the sex more like his favor to me, and the date is my favor to him. I mean, that's the opposite of how it's supposed to be for a player, right?

What am I not understanding about Lance Lightfoot?

I push my hair out of my face. "Yeah. Okay."

He hands me his phone and I enter my digits, fingers trembling slightly.

He takes it back and pockets it. "I'm leaving town tomorrow, but when I get back, we're going on that date." His dimples wink at me. He's so damn charming.

Oh. I shouldn't be so disappointed to find out it won't be soon. I shouldn't be disappointed at all.

"Where are you going?"

"Mm, that's classified, angel."

My brow furrows. "You're going on a mission?"

He gives a single nod.

I don't know why something drops to the pit of my stomach. I wasn't even counting Lance as a candidate for The Big Plan, but I hate that he's presumably in as much danger as my brother. Guys like him are adrenaline junkies. Here one day, gone the next, like my parents were when I was growing up.

"So you're still in the thick of it, aren't you?" I eye him, that quiver of anxiety I was feeling for Chad starting up now for him. "Your missions are as dangerous as when you were in the service?" When he hesitates, I see the truth. "Even more dangerous?"

He shrugs. "Let's just say when my brother decided our unit needed out, the government jumped at the opportunity to use us in ways they couldn't when we were in the armed forces."

Anxiety grinds harder.

Lance seems to see it, because he touches the place between my brows where I must be frowning. "You don't need to worry about us. We are specially equipped for this sort of work."

I swallow, not liking the taste of this. "I think that just means desensitized to danger."

Lance opens his mouth, then seems to think better of whatever he was going to say. He shrugs. "Something like that." He leans in, giving me a kiss on the temple. "You good? Did I satisfy you, or do you need another round?"

My laugh comes out husky. "You definitely satisfied me."

"There's more where that came from, angel." He winks, but when I wince, his cocky smile dips. "I'm good for more than sex, too, though," he says.

Huh. It doesn't quite compute. Why does it seem like Lance is looking for a girlfriend? He definitely doesn't strike me as the settling down type.

"One date," he says. "Promise me you'll stop judging me for one date. Then you can go back to all your assumptions about me if you want."

My lips part, a puff of breath coming out with my surprise. My face grows warm. "I'm sorry. I'm just confused about what this is."

Lance perches his hip against the arm of the sofa, looking sexier than a man has any right to. "Okay, can I be totally honest?"

I fold my arms across my chest, defending against the charm and whatever it is he's going to lay on me. "Please do."

"The truth is, I feel like I screwed up with you."

The shock of his statement makes something fluffy explode in my chest. Like if a dandelion suddenly turned to puff. "What do you mean?"

"I mean, I went into it for the hookup, you're right. But then I realized... " He chews the inside of his cheek, looking sideways. "I don't know, I felt like we had a real connection, and I wanted something more than a one-off. I wished I'd started this thing the right way."

"Wow. I don't know what to say." I nibble my lip. It's true we have a surprisingly easy—and uberhot—connection, but I was chalking that up to the fact that he wasn't a real relationship candidate for me. I'm just not sure I could switch him into that category. I mean, he's the opposite of what I'm looking for. The opposite of my man-plan. He's everything I made The Big Plan to avoid. He's probably an adrenaline junkie—addicted to speed, danger, and women. He's daring death with every dangerous mission he goes on.

"How do you feel about doing taxes?"

He shrugs. "I don't know. Never done them. Why?"

"No reason." This is not my guy.

But I don't have the heart to tell him that. I owe it to him to give him a chance.

Show up for our date with an open mind.

"Just say you'll give me a chance?" Lance shoves both his hands into his pockets, suddenly appearing far less cocky than usual.

I lean in and give him a peck on the lips. "Absolutely. I'm looking forward to our date."

It's not a lie.

Spending time with Lance is no hardship. I just don't want to lead him on…

CHAPTER 6

ADELE'S CHOCOLATE shop is gorgeous and tasteful, much like Adele herself. My beautiful friend is in one of her gorgeous outfits she wears so well—a silk blouse, and gray wool pencil skirt. She adds an apron when she cooks, but otherwise looks like a billion bucks. Like the CEO of a Swiss bank or a fashion company or something.

I'm in one of my t-shirts, a simple black one with the funny saying covered up by a pink and white apron. My boobs are swollen today, and the shirt feels a little tight. I've been volunteering at The Chocolatier to help Adele get ready for the holiday rush. Tabitha has also been putting in regular days, but had a jewelry show to visit today. Without her, the shop is quiet.

Which is good. Gives Adele and me time to talk in between customers. The strain I first noticed at my birthday dinner still pinches her forehead. The circles under her eyes are deeper, and her pale brown skin is a little less glowy.

"So what's really going on with you?" I finally blurt when the shop empties.

Adele raises a slim brow but keeps rearranging the specialty bags of pralines. "So what happened with that boy of yours? Mr. One-Night-Stand?" she volleys back.

I bite my lip. So that's how it's gonna be. Tit for tat. An equal exchange of information. "We hooked up."

"And you didn't tell me?" Adele straightens and leans on the counter. "How was it?"

"It was good." A flush works its way up my neck. "Really good."

"And you didn't tell me, why?"

I shrug. "Didn't want to make a big thing of it. I had fun. And then we hooked up again."

"I beg your pardon." Adele cups her ear. "Did you just say Mr. One-Night-Stand wanted another night?"

"I know, right?" The heat of the flush reaches my cheeks. "Who'da thunk?"

"Maybe the right woman will make him change his ways." She goes back to the pralines but lifts her head when I'm silent.

"Um, yeah, he actually wants to see me again. I think… he wants more. With me. I don't know what to do."

"And I'm just now hearing about this?" Now Adele's hands are on her hips. I'm in trouble.

"It was supposed to be a one-night stand!" I drop my head on the counter. "I didn't want to tell anyone because then it would feel too real."

"But he wants more."

"Yes," I groan.

"And you don't?"

"I... I don't know. The sex was great. I just... don't know if I can do it, you know? I mean, I'm at the age where I need to be looking for a life partner. Lance probably doesn't even know how to do taxes."

Adele blinks. "And that matters why?"

"No reason," I mumble. "I just thought it would be nice to marry someone who could also do our taxes."

"Well, maybe it's not so bad," Adele says slowly. "Have you asked him his opinion of farming cacti? Or ficus?"

When I raise my head, I catch the ghost of a smile on her face. "You're laughing at me," I grumble.

"Charlie, my Mémère had a saying: *We plan, God laughs.* I know you want life to unfold the way you imagined, but..."

"I know," I groan. "I know. I just wanted more stability for my life. Especially because I want kids." What would it be like to have kids with Lance? Immediately I imagine a gaggle of tow-headed kids, running circles around me. *Forget it,* logic intervenes. *Lance would run in the opposite direction from any responsibility.*

"All right," I say, heading around the counter so I can help stack bags of pralines on their display. "Your turn. I spilled my secret, now you spill yours."

"Fine." Adele sighs, accepting my abrupt change of subject. "It's Bing."

"Your business partner?" I wrinkle my nose. I've never met Bing officially but I've seen him around. He's a trustafarian—a particular type of Taos resident. No job; just a trust fund and rich parents, and a tendency to smoke pot and wear Bob Marley shirts. I don't know any trustafarians very well, because patchouli oil, especially when worn in place of deodorant, makes my eyes water.

"I think he's taking money from our account," Adele says. "I was supposed to pay rent last week. This is the third month in a row that I had it in the account and it disappeared. Before I could pay the landlord."

"Oh my God." My head spins. "Were you able to pay the rent?" This is prime real estate in Taos, right on the main tourist drag, near enough to the plaza that The Chocolatier gets foot traffic. Adele doesn't have to do much advertising but her rent is probably high.

"I paid it." Adele waves a hand. "I had to pull it from my own savings. And this is the third time."

I feel a little sick. "Adele, Bing is stealing from you."

"It's his money too," she says defensively. "He used to take draws from the account and tell me it was some sort of investment for the business but now he's given up all pretense. And I haven't even been able to get a hold of him."

"I'm so sorry," I say. I've never been interested in owning my own business (outside of a project in retirement). I've always been impressed by Adele's courage. She's so smart, and works so hard. "What can I do to help?" I ask.

"You already are helping," Adele says. "I thought by now I'd be able to hire a few people to help me run the shop. But with the money disappearing…" She gives her head a brisk shake. "And Bing is no help."

"No. It doesn't sound like Bing is a help at all. Quite the opposite." I want to say more but my gut is churning. Sadie or Tabitha would know exactly what to say—Sadie would be sweet, and Tabitha would make plans to hunt Bing's butt down and stake him out on a hill of fire ants until he promised to return the money.

I put my hand over my stomach, breathing deeply to calm the queasiness.

What are the next steps for Adele? A lawyer? What if she can't afford one? What if Bing steals so much that she goes out of business? Life won't be the same in Taos without The Chocolatier. And what will Adele do?

Before I can say anything, the bell over the door chimes and a customer walks in. She's a slim woman with ash blonde hair carefully styled, but her eyes are red and her mascara is smudged.

"I just drove up from Santa Fe. I want one of everything," she announces, and slaps a hand over her mouth too late to hold in her sob. She doubles over, putting her head right down on the counter in a position I'm all too familiar with.

"Oh, honey," Adele croons. She drops what she's doing and heads over to comfort the woman. I hover in the background, grabbing a big box and starting to fill it while still staying alert to help Adele with anything she needs.

"Tell me everything." Adele is in full on mothering mode. Within seconds, she has a little white china plate out and a few samples artfully displayed on a gold doily.

The customer sniffles and Adele is ready, handing the poor woman a fabric handkerchief.

"He's sleeping with the nanny," the woman wails, blotting up tears and runny mascara while Adele makes sympathetic noises. "I never would've figured it out but Barbara from tennis doubles told me. The witch."

Adele agrees without clarifying who the witch is: the nanny, or Barbara from tennis doubles. She motions to me to get a second pink and white box. I grab one and start filling it with the creme filled truffles.

"How could he do this to me?" the woman cries. "I just got my breasts done!"

After a half an hour, the woman has stopped crying and started plotting her revenge. Adele and I send her on her way with three bags full of boxes of chocolates, truffles, and pralines, but not before Adele makes the woman promise to talk to a lawyer before doing anything like throwing her husband's golf clubs into the river.

You've got to keep them away from their husband's golf clubs, she told me, Tabitha and Sadie once at a Whine Wednesday. *Bad things can happen. You don't want the cops to come knocking, trying to charge you with accessory to murder.*

"This happens a lot, doesn't it?" I murmur, twisting up a few white truffles into cute little Chocolatier branded bags.

"About once a week," Adele confirms.

"You're really good at it."

"I'm glad my psychology degree is coming in handy," she says with a wry smile, and we both laugh. Adele's parents wanted her to be a psychologist or some sort of doctor like them. It was her Mémère who gave her the seed money to open The Chocolatier. If I remember correctly, Bing put up the rest and called in a favor to get them a prime real estate spot to lease.

The chocolaterie can't fail. There's a knot in my throat when I tell this to Adele. I give her a hug, which she accepts, but she slants me a look when we break apart.

"Don't think I forgot how you changed the subject earlier. I want to know what you're going to do about Lance."

"Um, yeah. About that." I fiddle with a jar of toffees until Adele crosses her arms over her chest.

"Charlotte Louise." She sounds more motherly than my mother ever did.

"Fine," I say. "I'll talk it through with you, but only if I get to sample an Earl Gray truffle. I've had such a craving lately."

"Mmmhmm," she hums but grabs a second white china plate and gold doily.

A sound at the back of the shop makes us pause. The door

opens with a jingle—the back door. I look at Adele with wide eyes.

"Wait here," she mouths and races into the back. "Bing?" Her frosty tone carries to the front of the shop. "We need to talk." She sounds calm and professional, but I run to the front door and lock it anyway, flipping the sign to *Out for lunch*.

Then I run back to make sure Adele doesn't murder her partner.

Adele is already there, facing off with a middle-aged white guy. Bing the business partner has long hair tied back in a ponytail, and a faded Grateful Dead shirt that reeks of pot. Typically trustafarian.

"Christopher Eugene Ford," Adele says, and the man's gaze drops to his Birkenstocks. She blows out a breath and turns to me to explain, "His real name is Chris. But when he moved to Taos, he re-christened himself *Bing*."

I roll my eyes. Only in Taos. We've got lots of 'Jim' and 'Brenda's who've renamed themselves 'Zen' and 'Moonjuice'.

"Hey, Adele." The business partner formerly known as Christopher shuffles his feet. He looks like a kid caught with his hand in the chocolate jar.

"Do you have something for me?" Adele folds her arms over her chest. "Like the money for the last three months' rent?"

"Aww, yeah." He rubs the back of his neck. "I can get it to you. I just need—there's an investment I got caught up in and…" He trails off at the sharp tapping of Adele's booted toe.

I hold my breath, ready for her to tear into him.

But her shoulders slump. "This can't go on, Chris," she says, sounding exhausted. "If you keep taking big draws, we'll lose the business."

I step back into the front of the shop before I can hear Bing/Chris' mumbled reply. Now that I'm sure Adele won't kill him, I don't want to intrude on a private conversation. Besides, it feels wrong, seeing Adele so defeated.

I bite my lip, wondering if I should tell Sadie and Tabitha. I don't want Adele to go through this alone, but it's her business.

I wish there was someone neutral I could confide in. Someone who'd offer a strong shoulder to lean on, who's likely to care.

It's curious how the first person who comes to mind is Lance.

 antiago, Chile

Lance

"LANCE, can you hear me? I need you to say something." The tautness in Rafe's voice makes me open my eyes. Not because of the Alpha Command he used, but because I hear fear. A sound I can't stand hearing from our alpha.

From my brother.

I've only heard that tone one other time, and it was the worst day of both our lives.

"I hear you," I manage to wheeze.

This mission in Chile went sideways fast. It wasn't like the one in Switzerland last month, where we were on recon and were suddenly made. We still don't know how that happened—where the mole was. That was just a case of bad luck. Sometimes things go awry.

For this mission, we were sent in by the CIA to rob arms dealer Vincent Sarcero of his enormous stores of cash. Basically, our government hoped to cut him off at the knees and stop a huge deal before it could happen, by taking his capital. Why we couldn't just kill him wasn't divulged, but they wanted him alive, just rendered impotent.

We spent ten days scoping the place out and making our plan. Ten long days I was away from Charlie. My sweet female. The one I haven't claimed yet. Who barely agreed to one date with me.

We went in like it was a heist and we were high-end thieves. We mapped the place out, knew their security, and had a well-laid plan.

We got in without a hitch. The only problem was that we thought the safe would hold cash. Our plan was to set off a bomb inside, and burn it all to ashes.

But we were misinformed about the contents of the safe. It didn't hold cash. It housed gold bars. So we had to revise the plan on the fly, and pack that shit out of there. I suggested we abort and regroup—come back the next night with means to carry and transport the gold. Rafe made the call for us to continue. So our intended thirty minute operation turned into an all-night affair of repeated trips hauling gold bars out of the mansion. Fortunately, we're strong and fast. We'd done our homework on security. The guard dogs were tranqued; the security cameras were intercepted and shown a false feed.

But at five this morning, when the guards changed over, someone spotted our vehicle parked near the wall for loading.

The place went from dead quiet to war zone in a matter of sixty seconds. I was in the safe room, caught with my pants down.

I took a couple dozen rounds from a semi-automatic and

went down to play dead until I could shift and get the fuck out there.

The trouble was, the room didn't clear. More and more assholes kept coming in. I was gonna get stuck in there and bleed out before my wolf could heal me. I shifted, startling the men long enough to get through the door, but took another dozen rounds to my back as I fled the scene.

Deke and Rafe came for me, and had no choice but to kill the men who had seen me. Not at all the stealthy, quiet affair this was supposed to be.

Now we're racing away in the truck made too heavy by the gold bars I'm lying on, bleeding.

"For fuck's sake, how many bullets did he take?" Channing also sounds panicked.

I must look really bad.

"Too many." Again, it's the agony in Rafe's voice that opens my eyes.

"Not too many," I wheeze. "Just give me a minute."

"Why can't you shift?" Rafe demands.

Can't I? Why am I in human form? I don't even remember changing back. We heal faster in wolf form.

I try to shift, but Rafe's right. I can't.

"Command it," I mumble.

"You think I didn't fucking try that? *Shift.*" Rafe uses Alpha Command, which should trigger a biological response in me to immediately obey.

I barely register the command in my cells. For that matter, I'm barely registering my body.

"Was he shot in the head?" Deke's tinny voice comes from the comms. He must be driving the truck.

Someone moves my head around like he's inspecting it. "Fuck." It's Channing.

"*Was he?*" Rafe chokes. The panic in his tone once more

brings back our childhood trauma. The sound of our father's voice when he commanded us to shift and run. To hide.

The sound in Rafe's voice when we came back and found our parents' dead bodies.

"Yeah." Channing's modulating his voice to make it sound more casual. "But the bullet's already coming out, see?"

"*Shift*, motherfucker," Rafe commands again.

This time, my body obeys. I change into wolf form. The scent of my blood-matted fur offends my sensitive nose. I pant, severely weakened, but coming back to my body. I feel the pain, and also the healing.

"How is he?" Deke barks.

"He shifted." I hear the relief overlying in Rafe's still-stressed voice.

"Good. Now, how the fuck are we going to get rid of this gold?"

Rafe is silent for a long moment, then he commands, "Drive straight to the airport. We'll take a private plane."

"We're taking it with us?" Channing sounds surprised.

"I need to get Lance home to heal. You got any other ideas?"

"We could drive it out somewhere and bury it."

"I don't want to leave it anywhere where Sarcero can get his hands on it again. And I doubt he'll stop looking for it."

Dammit. That means Sarcero is still alive. I was hoping he'd been taken out in the melee.

"Maybe we can get U.S. Customs to seize it. Very publicly but without releasing our names. That way, he stops hunting. He may try to find us for revenge, but he won't think we still have it."

"Good idea, Channing, I like it," Rafe says.

I don't like any of it. Because I now have a female to

consider when I think about some arms dealer using every resource he has to hunt down the men he believes are thieves. In fact, I wish to fuck we had just gone in to take Sarcero out. I doubt the CIA would have cared, either way. It was probably Rafe's call to not get more blood on our hands than necessary.

I think he miscalculated.

~

Lance

Twenty hours later, we land in Taos. We stopped in Dallas to go through customs, where the gold was 'seized'—all prearranged by the CIA, and publicly blamed on a drug cartel.

I stayed in wolf form through all of that, scaring the shit out of a couple customs and CIA agents surprised to find our team used a very large drug and cash-sniffing war dog for operations. At least the guys had hosed the blood off me before I got on the plane.

Now that we're back, I shift into human form, in much better shape than I was a day ago.

Especially when I remember I have a date.

I pull on a pair of pants and t-shirt and reach for my phone to text Charlie. *I'm back in the country. Dinner tonight?*

Rafe narrows his eyes. "Who are you texting?"

"Don't pretend you don't know." I'm a little short on my usual good humor due to the residual pain in almost every part of my body.

"You can't see her," he warns.

He's my alpha, which means telling him to fuck off won't go over well. Still, I want him to fuck all the way off.

"I'm fine." It's a lie. It must be from the bullet to the head, or maybe just the sheer number of bullets I took, but my recovery has been slower than I'd like. My breath still wheezes, and I'm weak and sore all over.

"The fuck you are," Rafe snaps. "And you know you can't let her see you like that."

I raise a brow, because that's not true. If Charlie were some random human, yes. I couldn't let her witness my healing process. But Charlie is my mate. I plan to tell her what I am, just as soon as I don't think it will send her running. Still, Rafe is probably right. This wouldn't be the way I'd choose to tell her.

But the thought of delaying our date another day makes me want to punch a hole through the wall of this plane.

It turns out the point is moot, though, as we climb out of the plane. Charlie texts me back: *I'm not feeling great today —a stomach thing. Can we wait?*

Sure, I text back, but my wolf snarls at the idea of her not feeling well. The need to shift immediately and run straight to her makes me have to stop and close my eyes, drawing deep breaths into my still healing lungs.

"You okay?" Deke lays a giant ham-hand on my shoulder.

"Yeah. My mate isn't feeling well."

Fuck. I didn't mean to say that. I haven't told the rest of the guys about Charlie yet.

Deke's brows slam down. "What now?"

I shake my head. "Nothing. Nevermind."

"Uh-uh. You said *mate*. Who the fuck are you talking about?"

I grit my teeth. "She hasn't accepted me yet," I mutter.

"Who is it?" Deke demands, now attracting the attention of Channing, too. At least Rafe is off wrapping things up with the pilot.

"I need you both to shut the fuck up."

Channing folds his arms across his Hollywood pecs. "We're not moving until you spill."

"It's Charlie." I look at Deke, begging him for something, I don't even know what. He has a human mate. I'm hoping he'll somehow know how to save me from the agony I feel right now. I'm dying because I haven't claimed her. I'm dying because I haven't seen her in ten days. And I'm especially dying because now she's told me she's not feeling well.

My need to go and help her, to protect her, overrides all reason.

Deke's eyes widen. "Sadie's Charlie?" he asks.

"Yeah. We hooked up."

Deke's eyes narrow with doubt. "I don't know why the fuck you started any conversation about your mate with: *we hooked up*. Only you, asshole. Are you sure she's your mate? I mean…"

I snarl and fist his shirt, even though I'm in no condition for a tussle and I'd never win against Deke—he's huge. "You think I don't fucking know that?" I get my face right up in his grill. "I fucked it up royally. I didn't even recognize my own damn mate until I had her naked and beneath me, and now I don't know how to change her opinion of me."

Deke's expression softens to sympathy. "Aw, shit, Lance. You didn't."

I nod, miserable. "I did. My teeth came down to mark her and *then* I finally figured out why I'd been so hot to nail her."

"The lady-killer finally gets what's coming to him." Channing chortles.

I want to punch him in the face. "There is nothing fucking funny about this situation."

Channing smooths his smile down. "Right. I feel your pain, man."

"No," —I shake my head— "you don't. You don't have a fucking clue."

"Right. Well, that's true." Channing still looks like he's enjoying the hell out of this.

"Well, I'm sure it will all work out," Deke says, but doubt drips from his voice. "Maybe just try to get to know her before you get horizontal with her again."

"Yeah, no fucking duh." Great. I sound like a fourth grader. This female makes me lose all brain cells.

Rafe comes over, and we pick up our bags and hike off the tarmac to the parking lot where we left the Humvee.

"Drop me off somewhere I can shift," I tell Rafe, who slides behind the wheel.

"What? Why?"

When I don't answer, he twists in his seat to look at me. "No."

"Just let me out."

I hear his teeth grit, and a growl starts up in my throat.

I expect Rafe to really throw down with me, but he goes easy. "Seriously, dude? You're gonna stalk her mail route again?"

"Fuck you." Definitely still a fourth grader. I didn't know Rafe knew I'd been stalking her.

"Don't let anyone see you, asshole." He pulls off on the side of the road where I can disappear into the sage brush. "The only reason I'm letting you do this is because being in wolf form is the fastest way you'll heal."

I should say *thanks*, but since our parents' murder, his concern for me is suffocating. It's hard to always be the little brother. He bears all the responsibilities in the world. I hold none.

"See ya." I shift and run, my wolf practically frantic to catch Charlie's scent.

harlie

MY HANDS TREMBLE as I dump the contents of the plastic bag out on my bed. I just bought every brand of pregnancy test they had at Walgreens. I've been queasy for a couple days now, but I didn't think anything of it, not until I full-on puked on my route this morning and realized my period is also late.

Fuck, fuck, fuck.

I'm on the pill! This isn't supposed to happen. I mean, I was on the pill, and Lance used a condom. What are the chances of the condom slipping off *and* the pill being ineffective? Pretty freaking slim, I'm sure!

I draw a deep breath in and release it. Butterflies flap in my belly. Or maybe that's morning sickness.

This wasn't the plan. An accidental pregnancy with a player is the opposite of the plan.

He may not be a player, something whispers from beneath the layer of panic.

It did seem like he was trying to show me another side to him before he left. But he's still not stable. He's an operative in a highly dangerous field. Hardly the kind of father I wanted for my child.

I wanted safe. Predictable. Someone who wouldn't mind driving a minivan and doing our taxes.

Okay, I'm getting ahead of myself. This probably just a pregnancy scare. My mind running away with me. I read the instructions on all the tests. Even though you're supposed to wait for the first morning urination for best results, I take a stick to the bathroom right now, and pee on it.

Then I wait.

And hold my breath.

And wait some more.

Tears cloud my vision. Is that a second pink line coming in the window?

Oh shit. Is it? Oh my God.

It totally is.

I'm pregnant. This was not how I wanted it to happen! This was not the stupid plan!

Tears stream down my face. I pick up the phone and start to search for Adele, since she's the one who knows I hooked up with Lance, but instead I find myself calling Sadie.

I don't know why. I guess because she practically lives over at that compound with Lance due to how much time she spends at Deke's. She knows him—maybe better than I do. I can talk this through with her.

She picks up, and I have to hold in a sob.

"Sadie?"

"Charlie—how have you been, girl? I haven't seen you around." Is that a touch of guilt in her voice?

"I've been… busy. But—"

"Are you crying?"

"What?" I swipe my eyes. "No. Of course not." Maybe she'll think it's allergies or a cold or something.

"You don't sound okay."

"Yeah, I need to talk." This sucks. Saying it out loud makes it all the more real.

"Okay," she says slowly.

"I have a teeny tiny problem. You know Deke's friend— the hot blond one?"

"You mean Lance?" She sounds unsure.

"The one who looks like he could front a boy band," I say, which isn't fair. Lance is a playboy, but there's no boy about him.

"He's a bit more buff than that." I love how Sadie defends him. She sees the best in people.

"Okay, then, a Baywatch remake."

"I'll give you that." She giggles. "Lance does have a surfer-dude vibe going on. What about him?"

"We might have hooked up."

"Oh. Oh my. You and him?"

I hold back a half sob, half laugh. "Yeah. I know. It was on a whim."

"Good for you. I mean, it was good, right?"

"Better than good."

"I'm glad. So what's the problem?"

Ah, jeez. Now I have to explain. "It was supposed to be a one-time thing."

"Okay."

"Even though we really were great together."

"Okay..." Sadie sounds like she wants me to cut to the chase, but is too polite to say it.

"And now I have a problem." I swallow against the boulder in my throat before whispering the words, "I'm pregnant."

There's a pause. Then, "You are? Oh my God, Charlie! I'm excited for you!"

Oh jeez. This is why Adele would have been my first choice for a phone call. Sadie sees the best in every situation.

"Wait, is Lance the father?" Sadie is breathless. "Lance Lightfoot? Deke's Lance?" As if there's more than one Lance we know in Taos.

"Yeah. Can you believe it? I mean, the guy is a total man-whore, right?" I continue in a rush. "But it was my birthday and he's so sexy and persuasive, I figured it wouldn't hurt anything to enjoy myself for a change, you know? Just for fun. But the condom broke, and I guess the pill didn't work either, and now I'm pregnant!"

"Oh. Oh, I'm sorry, babe." Her voice softens. "Whatever you want, whatever you're feeling, I'm here for you."

I give a wild laugh. "I don't know. I guess I'm having a baby." Maybe if I say it out loud, I can believe it. "This wasn't exactly part of my life plan."

"I haven't had kids of my own yet, but I've heard so many mothers say that this is the one place you just can't control everything. You don't get to pick when you get pregnant, or the gender, or when they'll decide to be born. You have to sort of surrender."

Sadie is so sweet. It all makes sense, but I'm not even past the point of believing I'm pregnant. Thinking about the rest of childbearing is beyond me.

"So… what about Lance? When are you going to tell him?"

"I don't know. That's the thing. I mean, Lance isn't exactly the guy I had in mind to raise kids with."

"Why not?" There's no accusation in Sadie's voice, although she sounds perplexed.

"Well, the man-whore thing for one. And also—" I break

off because I don't want to add my worry to Sadie. I mean, she's already in deep with Deke. I wouldn't be surprised if they got married and had kids.

"Also, what?"

"Well, they're in a dangerous business. That's not really what I want for my family. I grew up worrying about my parents not coming home from their tours of duty. Now I worry about my brother. I don't want to have to worry about my hus—" I stop, because *husband* and *Lance* don't even seem to go together. "I mean, not that we're even going to be together. But we'll be co-parenting, I guess. I don't want to have to worry that my kid's dad won't come home from a mission."

"Listen, Charlie," Sadie says, sympathy lacing her words. "There's a lot you don't know about Lance, but he should be the one to tell you. You need to talk to him—right away."

"Yeah, I know…"

Not a conversation I'm even remotely ready to face.

"I mean, I'm terrible at holding in exciting news, so you have to tell him right away, or I'll burst."

I slap a hand over my forehead. "Sadie, please. Don't say anything to anyone. Not even to Deke."

"Um…" She sounds guilty.

"Is he right there?"

"Yeah, and he has really good hearing."

Dammit.

"Just talk to Lance. Right away, okay?"

My stomach quivers with anxiety. "Yeah, okay. I will. Thanks, Sadie."

I end the call, staring into space.

There's a lot you don't know about Lance, but he should be the one to tell you.

What does that mean? It wasn't what I'd hoped to get out

of the conversation. I'm not sure what I hoped—that she'd somehow know the one thing that would make all of this all right?

That doesn't exist.

Things aren't all right.

But I will have to work with what I've got.

I shriek when a knock sounds at my front door. Did Sadie call an emergency Whine Wednesday meeting already?

No, that's way too fast.

Oh God, I am so not up for company right now.

I jog for the door and throw it open, ready to tell whoever is there that now is not a good time.

But when I do, no sound comes out of my open mouth.

Lance is there, leaning against the doorframe, his brow in a deep furrow.

Lance

Charlie's new scent hits me, bowling me over like a tidal wave. I caught it today on the wind when I was following her. It's changed.

She's changed. Her breasts are swollen. Her face is stained with tears.

Fuck.

My female's pregnant, and she doesn't want it.

Misery washes through me, thick and hot.

I showed up on her doorstep, but words elude me.

"Lance." She sounds breathless, in a shocked way.

"Hey."

Hey—really? That's all I can think to say?

She doesn't move back to invite me in, even though cold

air fills her house, making her nipples protrude under her long-sleeved t-shirt.

"I don't want to disturb you, but, ah, I wanted to make sure you're okay."

She swallows. "Um. No, not really. But it turns out, it wasn't the stomach flu—I'm pregnant," she blurts.

I drop my head at the tears I hear in her voice. "I know," I say softly.

"You know?" She cocks her head.

I nod. "Yeah, I smelled it on you. Can I come in? There's something you need to know about that baby you're carrying."

Charlie's green eyes go wide and round.

This was so not the way I wanted to tell her. *Your baby isn't human* is the last thing you want to tell your baby-mama. And also, *baby-mama* is right up there with things I should never, ever have to say.

Mate is the only acceptable term.

Dammit.

"Okay," Charlie says, paranoia tinging her voice.

Great. I'm already scaring her.

I step into her entryway and take off my leather jacket.

"Did you say *you smelled it*?" She sounds incredulous.

"Yeah." I take a deep breath, words still failing me. "You know that wolf you've been seeing on your route?"

"What? How did you know about that?" Charlie takes mincing steps backward, completely confused.

I lift my palm up, facing her. "That's me."

She stops breathing.

I reach out to catch both her hands, afraid she's going to pass out.

"I'm so fucking sorry. This is not how I planned to tell you."

She stares up at me with those clear green eyes. "Um... I.... what?" Her hands are clammy, and she tries to pull them out of my grasp.

"I'm a wolf shifter. It's not an infection, we're a species. So your baby—our baby—will be half-shifter."

Charlie starts to laugh hysterically. "Oh my God." More giggles.

I release her hands and she stumbles backward, covering her mouth.

"What are you talking about? The wolf... " She goes still, dropping her hands away and staring at me like she just now understands. "You're the wolf on my route?"

I nod. "Listen, Charlie. You know how I said I started things all wrong?"

"Oh, we're way past all wrong, Lance." Charlie throws both hands in the air, turning and pacing away.

"Yeah, I know. See, the thing is, I didn't fully catch your scent at the hot springs. No, that's no excuse." Fuck. I'm not even making sense, and Charlie's already freaking out. "This is what I want to tell you. Wait. Can we sit down? Or—come here." I catch Charlie's waist to pick her up and sit her on her sturdy dining room table. My hands lightly rest on her hips. I just need to be touching her, have her close. I know she doesn't seem to want it, but my wolf is frantic.

Her eyes are even rounder than before. "Whoa. So you're really strong."

That wasn't what I was trying to show her. I shake my head. "Sorry. I don't want to scare you."

"Scared is not the emotion I'm feeling. Freaked out. Hysterical. Out of my mind... those all come closer."

I suddenly I catch the scent of her arousal.

What? She's turned on? She's distraught and confused but... apparently still likes to be manhandled by me.

Taking it as a sign her body knows me as her mate, even if she doesn't see it yet, I step in close, between her open knees. She's in a pair of faded grey leggings that show off her toned legs. I brush the backs of my fingers over her cheek. "I know you think I'm a player. You probably think I'm not father material for our baby."

"Our *wolf* baby." Her tone definitely suggests she thinks she's out of her mind.

"Wolf pup, yes."

She blinks.

"Anyway, you're not wrong—I was a player. That was totally me. But what you should know is that wolves mate for life. We have one mate who we know by instinct, and once we find that mate, we never leave. We'll do anything to protect and provide for our mate. To keep her satisfied and make her happy."

Charlie's face shows her obvious disbelief over what I'm telling her.

"You know how I said I screwed up?"

She nods.

"I'm such a jackass, I didn't figure out you were my mate until I was balls deep in you." I shake my head. "I honestly never expected to find my mate. It's a pretty slim chance of ever finding your true mate, and I wasn't thinking she'd be a human." I slide my hands up and down the outsides of her thighs. "What I'm trying to say and doing a terrible job of, is that you're my mate, Charlie. Pregnancy or not, there's no getting rid of me."

Her soft lips part and she stares into my eyes, almost as if mesmerized. "Lance… I can't digest this."

"Obviously, this is not how I intended to tell you. I mean, I was going to take you on that date."

Her hysterical laughter bubbles up again.

"Right. Our date." Her lower legs loop around behind my ass and she pulls me closer. "This is so weird." Her arms come up around my neck.

I wrap her up in mine and hold her. "Please give me a chance, Charlie. I want to be your man in every way—a father to our pup, the guy who makes you scream to the rafters, the one you can always count on."

She lifts her cheek from my chest. "I'm having a wolf pup?" There's a trace of amusement in her tone now. Or maybe it's joy.

I smile tentatively. "Half-shifter. We won't find out until puberty whether they can actually shift or not."

Charlie suddenly gasps. "Is Deke a werewolf too?"

I nod.

"So that's what Sadie meant when she said there's a lot I don't know about you."

I let out a rueful chuckle. "Probably, yes. Does she know?"

Charlie nods. "So what does this mean? Will the pregnancy be different?"

I shove my fingers through my hair. I'd spent the evening researching it. "I don't think so. You can go ahead with normal gynecological care. They shouldn't detect anything different about our baby because it's in his or her human form. If anything, it will be a safer pregnancy than most because my species has regenerative healing properties."

Charlie sits a little taller, her palms stroking down my pecs. "You do?"

My dick punches out. Was that a purr in her voice?

"Uh-huh."

"And you're extra strong?"

Definitely a purr.

"Shifter strength. Yeah. Good stamina, too." I wink.

She smiles. "This is so crazy."

"Not as crazy as I am for you."

She shakes her head, but she's still smiling. "You don't even know me."

I sober. "I want to. Charlie, I really want to. Will you let me?"

"Of course," she relents, shoulders sagging. "Whether we become a thing or not, you're the father of this child."

Whether we become a thing or not.

She's still resisting me. I need to find out what her objections are, and break them down.

I run the backs of my fingers lightly down the front of her throat. "You still feeling sick?"

Our gazes lock. She shakes her head slowly. "Not at the moment." Her voice is husky.

"Can I make you feel good? Help you burn off a little stress?"

She unbuttons my jeans. "With this?" She reaches in and gives my hardened dick a squeeze.

A shudder of pleasure runs through my entire body. "Yeah," I choke.

"Can I see your wolf first?"

"Anything for you, angel. But why?"

"I just want to see him up close."

I cup her cheek. "I'm sorry I scared you that time. I never should have let you see me."

"Oh, I saw you lots of times," she boasts. "I was playing spot the wolf on my route every day."

I grin. "I couldn't stay away." I strip off of my shirt, forgetting about my wounds, and she gasps. "Lance! Oh my God."

"No, no, no, no." I wave my hands. "Don't freak out. I got shot a couple days ago, but these will be gone by tomorrow. I promise. Nothing to worry about. Normally they'd be gone already, but I took quite a few bullets at once."

"Quite a few," she repeats dazedly, still covering her mouth in horror.

Not wanting her to look at them any longer, I strip out of my jeans and boxers, and shift.

"Lance," she breathes again, this time reaching for me. I lift my head to place it between her knees, and she rubs my ears. "So soft. Oh my God, your fur is so soft. So beautiful. And terrifying. I mean, you are huge."

That's what I've been told. I wag my tail.

She rolls her eyes like she knows what I'm thinking. "I didn't mean it that way. Although, you are pretty well-endowed in the package department, too."

I lick her fingers.

"So our baby… will be like this?"

I shift back, covering my erection with one hand. "If they get enough of the shifter gene. Some halflings never shift." I grip both her knees. "You gonna let me between these sweet thighs of yours now?"

"Let's go to the bedroom."

"As you wish." I scoop her easily up to straddle my bare waist, and carry her to the bedroom, where I make sure every inch of her body receives the pleasure she deserves.

harlie

THE SCENT of coffee in the morning strangely doesn't turn my stomach. Maybe it was all that 'stress-relief' last night. I mean, all that extra oxytocin released with the multiple orgasms probably helps everything, right?

It's hard to remember now why I was so resistant to Lance. One minute he was this cocky playboy I let into my pants, and the next minute, he's telling me he's a wolf—*a wolf!*—and that I'm his mate. That he's going to dedicate his life to making me happy.

It's all too crazy, but those flapping wings of anxiety are mostly gone from my belly. I don't know if I can really believe he's the reformed player, but I can admit he's making a concerted effort to prove that to me.

I can't really ask for any more than that at the moment.

I climb out of bed. I'm naked, but the house seems very warm for November. I find Lance has built a fire in the kiva fireplace in my living room. He's standing in my kitchen in his boxer briefs, cooking on the griddle.

"Hey, beautiful." He sends a panty-dropping smile over his shoulder. Seriously. The man should not be so lethally good-looking. "I know you've been queasy, but I've been researching, and it sounds like not letting your belly get empty is the key to avoiding morning sickness. Counter-intuitive, but the internet swears by it." Another lust-inducing grin.

"What are you cooking?"

"Your choice. I have pancakes; a spinach, tomato, and cheese omelet; or I could do French toast."

"Omelet," I say, my mouth watering. A hint of queasiness washes over me. I'll test his research and see if the food makes it worse or better. It's true I skipped breakfast yesterday when I didn't feel hungry. Maybe that's why I puked. "This is sweet of you," I say, taking the plate he hands me.

"Get used to it. I literally won't be able to rest if I don't think you're taken care of."

I stare at him. "This is so… weird."

"Also, if you don't put some clothes on, you're gonna get fucked again. Hard." He flicks his brows at me and lowers his gaze to his briefs, where his cock has tented the soft cotton.

I hesitate, calculating whether I want to eat or have Lance's hands on me again.

"Eat," he insists. "I want you well-nourished before I ravish you." He gives me one of those winks.

I run my fingers over his torso. He was right—the bullet wounds have faded significantly. The guy does heal fast.

He groans at my touch. "Eat," he murmurs. "Please."

I sit down and take a bite of the omelet. "Mmm. Delicious." The food does seem like what my body needs.

I watch Lance go back to my kitchen, making cooking look like the most masculine task ever invented. I feel myself wanting to resist him still. Because it's hard to believe this is really what he says it is. That he's in it for life with me. Dedicated to making me happy.

And yet... when I think about Sadie with Deke, it's the same. Deke doesn't take his eyes off Sadie if she's in his presence. Ever.

"Is Sadie Deke's mate?" I ask, my mouth still full of omelet.

"Yes. Thank fuck. Deke was close to going feral before he found her."

I pause in scooping up my next forkful. "What do you mean?"

Lance brings a plate piled high with food—I mean, *heaped*—and sits down beside me to eat. "Dominant wolves can run into trouble if they don't find their mate in time. Their wolf goes mad and takes over. It's probably where humans derived the distorted legends about werewolves from." Lance shoves a giant forkful of eggs into his mouth.

I eye his plate. "Are you going to eat all of that?"

He flashes that Hollywood-worthy grin. "Yep. We eat a lot."

"No wonder you feel like you have to worry about providing for your female. Biologically, I mean."

His eyes are soft on me. "Yeah. Totally."

"Don't worry, I don't eat that much."

His laugh is rich and warm, and it sends shivers of pleasure down to my toes. "Angel, I wouldn't worry if you ate like a horse."

"Or a wolf."

He winks. "Right."

"So once you find your mate, you're obsessed with taking

care of her, and if you don't, you go mad? Sounds like a win-win for the female species." I reach over and take a forkful of his enormous stack of pancakes.

"Eh. We are a species that's going extinct. Maybe that's why Fate matched Deke and me with humans. Diversify the genes a bit."

I shake my head. "I'm really not sure I believe in the Fate-matched thing."

Lance shrugs his muscled shoulders. "Fate. Biology. Call it what you will. The instinct is real. Even if I was stupid enough not to recognize it the first time I saw you. In my defense, you were immersed in water, so I didn't get the full notes of your scent."

I smile, the memory of our first meeting even sweeter now that I know him better. I'd liked him then, in spite of my better sense. Now that I'm getting to know more about him, I like him even more.

"What you don't know is that I leapt off the rock above you in wolf form." He flashes a pirate grin. "I didn't know you were in there, and had to shift mid-air."

I clap my hand over my mouth, laughing. "Oh no, that's hilarious. Well, you surprised the heck out of me, too."

"A pleasant surprise, I hope." His eyes grow soft.

"Very pleasant," I murmur. "One of my best birthdays ever, I have to say." My hand slips to my belly. Despite the fact that this pregnancy was unplanned, it doesn't diminish what a gift it is. I've always wanted children. Always planned to have a family.

I glance at the clock and pop the last bite of omelet in my mouth. "I'd better get going. I can't be late to work."

"Of course not. I don't mean to delay you."

I stand and lean in to kiss his temple. He lets out a distinctly animal-like growl, his hands coming to my bare waist. I suppose my breasts swinging near his face are a bit of a temptation. "Want to help me shower?" My voice turns husky.

Lance shoots out of his chair, picking me up by the waist and swinging me into a honeymoon carry. "I promise I'll get you to work on time," he swears as he swiftly walks me to the bathroom.

I laugh, warmth sliding through me.

A voice in the back of my head tells me not to get used to this. Not to get attached. Things might not work out.

They probably can't last.

But I've had enough emotional upheaval for one week, finding out I am pregnant and then finding out I'm having a wolf for a baby. I think I deserve to ignore the overprotective voice for the moment.

I can figure out how to re-plan the plan tomorrow.

Lance

Rafe gives me the side-eye when I come into the living room smelling like Charlie's shower gel. I probably smell like Charlie, too, even though I took care of her needs under the spray of water.

Rafe is at the computer desk in the corner.

"How's it going with the human?"

If I hadn't just had the release of sex with Charlie, I'd probably tackle him. I stop still and pin him with a look. He's four years older, and has been in charge of me since the day our parents gave their lives to save ours. I don't push back often, but when it comes to my mate, my wolf won't back down. "Don't ever call her *the human* again," I say with enough menace to make Rafe flick his brows. "Her name is

Charlie. You will call her Charlie. I'm going to invite her over to meet all of you, and I expect you to be the fucking welcome-wagon."

"So you've marked her?"

I growl. It's like my wolf thinks Rafe's moving in on her before I can, which, of course, is asinine. "Not yet." I haven't even told her about the marking thing. She had enough to digest with the 'your baby isn't human' thing.

"Right." Rafe rubs his face. "Exactly how do you see this all playing out, Lance? You think you're mate material? With the life we lead? How will you even get this girl to take you seriously?"

A hot flush of shame pushes through me. I turn away so he won't see that he's getting to me. Rafe is poking me where it hurts, because no one takes me seriously. I've made sure of that by taking the part of the playboy. The goof-off. The womanizing asshole who never takes anything too seriously.

I suppose it was to counterbalance Rafe, who takes every-thing way too fucking seriously. Including my own mating.

"She's a woman, not a girl." I'm getting testier by the minute. "And I'm going to figure that out."

"You're sure she's your mate?"

"She's my mate, and she's pregnant with my pup."

Rafe's jaw goes slack for a moment, then he surges to his feet, his work at the computer forgotten. "What?"

I square off against him, my shoulders set. "You heard me."

"What happened to your protection?"

Oh, for fuck's sake. He still thinks I'm fifteen and need him to counsel me about always wearing a goddamn rubber. "It came off. Because she's my fucking mate, and my wolf wanted to mark her. Do you want all the details?" I ask sarcastically. "The position we were in? The number of times

I made her come? Because you are seriously way too up in my business right now."

"You starting a family is everyone's business, Lance," Rafe snaps, striding over to me. His eyes flash amber, showing his wolf. "We are soldiers for hire on the most dangerous operations in the world, and you think it's a good time to knock up a hu—" He wisely stops before I punch him in the nose. "—your female?"

I rub a hand over my closely-cropped hair. "I already told you, it was an accident. There was no *thinking about starting a family.* My wolf wanted to claim her. It was all I could do not to sink my teeth in her neck and lose her forever."

That thought brings a little more control back. I have a human female. I will require so much more control than ever to make sure I never hurt or harm her. When I mark her, I will have to be sure I'm in total awareness and control, because fucking up could mean I hit an artery and she bleeds out.

Rafe sobers, too, his eyes returning to their human color. "Lance, this is a problem," he says quietly.

"Why?"

"How are you going to keep them safe?" It's only the haunted quality to Rafe's eyes that keeps me from taking offense.

Because we were orphaned by the most alpha of parents, who died to keep us from getting picked up by shifter slavers. Because Rafe has feared losing me the way we lost them since the moment he took charge of me at the tender age of fifteen. Because Rafe carries the weight and responsibility of keeping everyone in our small pack safe, and that will be infinitely harder if there are pups involved.

I force myself to swallow under the tight band around my throat. "I will keep them safe," I tell him. "It's not on you."

"Of course it's on me," he explodes. "It may be only a

matter of days before Sarcero cuts through the bullshit story the CIA built, and uncovers our identities. He's gonna want revenge, which ordinarily, I wouldn't worry too much about, but I just saw you take thirty rounds and nearly not make it out, and you're a fucking shifter. How the hell are we going to keep Charlie safe from a man like that? How are we going to keep that unborn pup safe?"

Fear strikes me at the base of my spine. Real fear. The kind I felt when we were running for our lives through those woods, our father's command still ringing in our ears.

Charlie and my pup are in danger right now. Just by my existence. If anyone ever linked them to me, they'd be used as leverage. Or maybe just butchered for revenge. And we probably have more enemies out there than Sarcero. There might be hundreds of people who want us dead after the things we've done for our government.

"Dammit." Rafe paces away from me. "I got us out of active duty to give us some breathing room, but it may have been my worst decision yet."

I stare at my brother in surprise. Fuck, I didn't know he second-guessed his decisions so much. He hides his doubt and vulnerability under his gruff, take-charge sergeant persona, but I can see it crumbling.

I also see how much we're in this thing together. He and I, same as it's always been. "Is a pup really the worst thing to happen to our family?" I ask softly. I haven't said the word *family* to him since we lost ours. I've never called us that. He and I haven't been family; we've been survivors. Fighters. Super-warriors for our government. We were pack, but not family. But it's clear he feels as responsible for my pup as I do, because he always carries the weight of responsibility for me.

When Rafe's gaze swivels to me, I see it holds a world of

pain. For a long moment, he doesn't answer, then he turns away. "No. Maybe not." His voice sounds a little more gruff than usual.

The image, suddenly, of Rafe as an uncle, not the gruff, hardened alpha he's become, fills my mind. "Maybe this pup is exactly the thing we've been missing," I suggest.

"I don't know, Lance." Rafe sounds exhausted. He walks out of the room, leaving his worry over my unborn child to fester in me.

Charlie

Lance picks me up in a Humvee after work. He wants me to come out to see the pack's compound and meet them all properly. It feels crazy and too soon, but well, this baby was crazy and too soon, so I guess the timing's right.

He showed up on my route again today in the usual place, but this time he trotted beside me like a giant guard dog. It took me a few minutes to shake the instinctive fear of such a large and ferocious-looking animal, but I very quickly found his presence to be a huge comfort. It also helped me believe everything I learned last night.

Lance really is a wolf. I'm having a wolf baby.

I should call my parents, but I'm not even remotely ready. It's way too new and weird. I don't even know how I feel about Lance. About our situation.

No, that's not true. I don't know what I *think*.

I do know how I feel.

I feel like I'm tumbling down a mountain, limbs flailing, with no plan, no parachute, but I have this guy beside me. This guy whose pirate smile makes me feel warm and gooey inside. This guy who makes me feel like maybe we could wing it, and still be all right. He's relaxed enough for both of us.

Except then my mind starts tumbling again. Lance may be relaxed, but that doesn't mean he should be. He's in an extremely dangerous profession. One that will keep him away from us for weeks at a time. Yes, he's essentially bullet-proof, but what if he's captured? Becomes a prisoner of war?

Lance glances over at me. "What's going on in that beautiful head of yours?"

I shake my head. "Just so much to digest."

"You looked worried."

For a player, he's awfully in tune with me. "Have you had a girlfriend before?" I blurt before I realize I'm not sure I want to hear the answer.

He gives me a sidelong glance, a slight smirk playing around his lips. "Never."

His answer doesn't surprise me, but my relief does. "Never ever? You're just a love 'em and leave 'em type?"

"Am I in trouble here?"

He's so damn sexy when he calls me on every single thing. I shake my head. "No. I was just wondering how you're so good at reading me."

The smirk returns. "You're my mate. It's my job, angel." Then his brows go down. "So you are worried."

I shrug. "I didn't want to marry into the military."

Confusion flits over his handsome face. "I'm out, angel."

"Are you, though? Really? It seems to me like you're still in the most dangerous aspect of the job."

"And you don't have to worry about me," he says with total confidence.

"What about the long trips?"

Lance's expression grows solemn. "I will never be away if you need me. I promise you that."

I chew on the inside of my cheek.

He reaches over and takes my hand. "Hey," he says softly. "Don't write me off before we've even had a go, okay? Give me a chance to show you I can be what you need me to be."

"And what is that?"

"That's what I'm trying to figure out."

I laugh in spite of myself. It's really impossible to keep Lance shut out. He's too persistent. Too perfect.

"Is there anything else I should know?"

Lance is silent a moment too long.

"What is it?" My pulse has already quickened.

Lance rubs the back of his neck. "Ah, yeah. There is something. I didn't want to freak you out last night."

"Already freaked," I say, putting my hands in the air.

He winces. "Okay, here it is. When a wolf mates his female, he marks her. With his teeth."

"Excuse me?"

Lance trails his index finger on a line from my neck to my shoulder. "Usually here. On a shifter, it's nothing. It would heal right up. On a human…"

"We're not doing that," I say immediately.

Lance goes quiet.

After a moment, I can't take the silence. "Lance?"

"If I don't mark you, my wolf could get frantic." He winces some more. "It's a biological urge, you know. To make sure no other male tries to move in on you."

I let out a *pfft*. "That's ridiculous."

"I know," he groans. "But it's real. Every minute I'm with you without claiming you, my wolf grows more restless. There's a possibility I could lose control, which would be bad." He looks across the cab at me. "Really bad."

I shift in my seat. "Okay, you're freaking me out."

"Yeah. That's why I didn't tell you last night. I figured the whole *I'm a wolf thing* was enough for one big reveal."

Once more, he wrenches a smile from me. "Okay, wait a minute. So how does biting me tell other males I'm yours, anyway? Like, they recognize your teeth marks or something?"

Lance chuckles. "My scent. The bite would embed my scent in you."

I shiver. "I don't like it."

"Yeah." He looks so miserable, I reach out to touch his leg.

"Just give me a little more time to assimilate all this, okay?"

"Of course." He sounds relieved.

I want to crawl in his lap and kiss his neck. Never in twenty million years would I have believed a guy like Lance would be hanging on my every word, my every look. Needing something from me—no, needing everything from me.

It's a strange, exotic power that I still can't believe I have, and that I innately know is somehow precious and sacred.

I don't understand the bond Lance feels with me, but I do believe it's real. I believe in him.

Lance parks in front of what looks like a million-dollar ski lodge. Nestled behind a river and up against the pine trees, it's the only building for miles around, which is probably why the pack picked it.

"This is idyllic. Do you own the place?" I ask.

"Yep." Wow. Okay, they must have quite a bit of money. I guess private sector security pays much better than straight military work.

"Do you guys ski?"

Lance nods. "Sure." He opens his door and gets out, then walks around to take my hand as I climb out of my side.

"Cross country or downhill?"

A shrug. "Both." He says it like it's nothing. There's probably no sport these guys don't excel at. They are super-human, after all. But it tells me they didn't buy the place for its proximity to the ski mountain. Or rather, they did— but not to ski. Probably to run and hunt.

"Oh my God, do you hunt?"

Lance stops and looks at me warily. "Like, with guns? No."

A semi-hysterical laugh bubbles out of my throat. "With your teeth?"

A wicked smile stretches his sensual lips. He shrugs. "It's in our nature." He wraps an arm behind my neck and tips my face up to his, lowering his lips. "Does it bother you?" The words aren't special, but his voice is a velvety caress that licks me right between the legs.

"I-I guess not."

He brushes his lips over mine, then nips at my lower lip. "Come in." He leads me up the wooden stairs.

I hesitate at the door. "Are they going to like me?"

"Rafe is pissed at me for doing this all wrong, but he would kill or die for you."

I stare at him with wide eyes. "Your brother?"

He nods. "Our alpha. So that means they all would. I promise." He pushes the door open, and ushers me in.

～

Lance

. . .

I TOLD the pack I was bringing Charlie over tonight, and it looks like they went to the effort of looking presentable. Rafe smells freshly showered. Channing has the grill going out on the deck outside the kitchen, flipping burgers.

Sadie's here with Deke, which instantly puts Charlie at ease. The two women hug and start to chatter away as Sadie unwraps a giant salad she brought. It's a gourmet one—the kind with spinach and pears and candied pecans. She pulls out a container of gorgonzola cheese and shakes it over the top while she asks Charlie a dozen questions about how she's feeling.

Deke nudges me with his elbow. "I don't know if I'm officially supposed to know yet, but congratulations," he says in a low voice.

A simultaneous ripple of pleasure and ferocious protectiveness runs through me. I almost can't speak for a moment. "Yeah, thanks."

Channing steps inside, holding a plate heaped with two dozen burgers. "Congratulations for what?" he demands, looking from me to Charlie. He lifts his nose in the air and sniffs, then looks puzzled. "You didn't clai—"

"Would you shut up?" I snap. For fuck's sake. I only just told Charlie about the claiming bite two minutes ago. What if I hadn't even mentioned it yet?

"Testy." Channing shakes his head, then cocks his brows at Charlie. "He's been like that ever since you two—"

"Please don't finish that thought," I interrupt, pinching the bridge of my nose.

Charlie seems amused, though. "Oh really? He's been Mr. Charming with me."

"Oh, he's always Mr. Charming," Rafe interjects, popping the lid off a Wolf Ridge IPA and offering it to our guest. "That's what he does best."

I snatch the beer out of his hand. "She doesn't want beer. I mean—" I turn apologetically to Charlie and backpedal— "A half a beer wouldn't hurt." She may like me bossy in bed, but I somehow doubt she's the kind of woman who takes kindly to being told what to do. "It's up to you, of course."

Charlie waves it off. "Nope. It's bad enough I was on the pill for a couple weeks before I realized I was pregnant."

"Pregnant!" Channing explodes, finally catching up. "For Fate's sake, why am I always the last to hear the news? And you haven't marked her y—"

"*Shut up, Channing.*" This time Deke joins me to make it a chorus. I guess the guy has some sympathy for me, being the only mated wolf here.

"I'll make us mocktails," Sadie chirps, moving to the refrigerator and pulling out a bottle of seltzer water and lemonade.

Rafe's lips tighten, like he's still stressed by the increased responsibilities he thinks he needs to take on with this pup.

"Yeah, I don't know about this whole marking thing. Sadie's going to have to give me the scoop. Later. *Privately.*" Charlie shoots a warning glance Channing's way. I love that my female is no shrinking violet.

Still, I'm starting to think bringing her here tonight was too soon. The pack is way too much for someone who didn't know shifters existed two days ago.

"I'm sorry." I touch her lower back, standing behind her. "The pack tends to think one wolf's business is every wolf's."

"Well, it sort of is," Rafe reminds me. "Your actions affect all of us."

Fuck.

Charlie's eyes narrow at Rafe. "That sounded a little judgmental."

Rafe's beer stops halfway to his lips and for a brief

moment, I think there's going to be a fight. Because there's no way I wouldn't defend my female if Rafe didn't answer nicely, even if he is our alpha.

But Rafe's not a dick. "I'm sorry," he says. "I didn't mean it to be. I know the pregnancy was an accident, and I'm thrilled for you both. For all of us." He lifts his beer, but the tightness around his eyes and mouth bely the gesture and the words.

Sadie lifts her glass of—something beautiful and girly—a fizzy lemonade with strawberry and mint garnish—and clinks it to Charlie's identical one. "I'm so freaking excited."

Deke wraps his arms around his sweet kindergarten teacher from behind, and kisses the top of her head. "She is. She's been talking non-stop about being a godmother. I hope you're planning on asking her."

Charlie's hand goes to her abdomen and she gives a weak laugh. "I haven't thought that far ahead, but of course Sadie would be my number one pick." She darts a glance my way. "Is that okay?" She shrugs with a comically exaggerated helpless look on her face.

"We don't do godparents, so it's all you on that call. The way wolves work, the entire pack will consider themselves godparents. That's all Rafe meant earlier." I shoot my brother a look to let him know that he's toast if he offends my female again.

"I just wish Lance had taken this all a little more seriously, that's all," Rafe mutters. "A mate and pups is a huge responsibility."

Charlie frowns. "Are you saying Lance isn't serious, or up to the responsibility?"

I barely suppress the growl in my throat—only for Charlie's sake. I don't want her to think it's directed at her. But

Fates, I would like to sink my teeth into Rafe's hide right now.

"I didn't say that," Rafe backtracks. "Lance performs well with any task. I have no doubt he'll make a great father and mate. I just didn't see this coming."

"*None of us did*," I growl, then scrub a hand across my face.

Charlie turns her frown on me and my stomach drops, but then she steps into my side, resting one hand on my chest and wrapping an arm behind my back. "Seriously. If you want to be part of this pregnancy, I need you all to be one hundred percent positive. Otherwise, we're doing this with my posse."

We're doing this.

It's only the fact that she said 'we' and seemed to claim me before she spoke that keeps me from tearing down the walls.

"You heard her." I put enough growl in my voice to warn all my pack brothers.

All three of them hold up their hands in surrender. No smart wolf would get between a wolf and his female.

"Charlie, we are at your disposal." Channing bows like an idiot. "We promise to be one hundred percent positive, all the way."

"Yep," Deke concurs.

"Apologies," Rafe says. "We were supposed to make you feel more comfortable with the pack tonight, and I think I fucked that up."

A huge layer of tension in my shoulders eases, especially when Charlie says, "It's fine. Just setting boundaries."

"She's very good at boundaries," Sadie says. "Now, let's eat, the burgers are getting cold."

"Yes, I'd better." Charlie looks up at me like she remembers my advice not to get hungry, and it does something wonky to my chest. I rush to pull out a chair for her, and grab a plate from the stack in the middle of the giant natural-edge maple table—my only contribution to our place, and the one piece of furniture I truly love.

Charlie runs her fingers over the gleaming surface, appreciatively. "This is beautiful," she murmurs.

It means everything to me that she appreciates it. I immediately want to dismantle it and bring it to her house for her to enjoy. Or will she move in here? Fuck, there's so much to figure out before the pup comes.

"Thanks. I bought it from a woodworker I befriended in Arroyo Seco. He does incredible work."

"He really does. I love it."

I heap her plate with food first, offering everything there is like she's in danger of starving to death any second. Only when she tucks into her food can I think about filling my own plate.

$\sim$

Lance

After dinner, I ask Charlie to stay, and bring her to my bedroom on the upper floor. I have a loft with an A-frame room. The west wall is floor-to-ceiling windows, looking out into the snowy forest. The sun set hours ago, but the moon has risen to bathe the forest in her pale light.

"Lance, this is incredible," Charlie breathes. "The view!"

"Yeah, I love it," I admit. The floors are polished oak and my furniture is simple, clean-lined wood. A large geometric-patterned rug in turquoise and brick covers the floor.

"What do you do in the morning, though? Doesn't the sun wake you up?"

I grin. "Yeah. I don't mind. I'm an early riser. I'll keep your head covered with a sheet in the morning."

Charlie smiles and rests both her hands on my chest. "What's the deal with your brother? Is he upset about the pregnancy?"

I cover her hands with mine. "No," I say, but the interaction doesn't sit well in my mind, either. I don't want Charlie to think any of it is about her, or the pup. I don't want her to dislike Rafe or feel unwelcome in our pack. I also don't like letting things get heavy. But it seems necessary.

"I should tell you something," I say.

She studies my face. "What is it?"

"Honestly, I don't think I've ever told this story before. I think Channing and Deke know most of it, but it's not because I've talked."

Charlies brows draw together in concern. "What is it?"

I turn to look out the giant window into the dark outline of trees, lit by moonlight. "Rafe and I were orphaned when I was eleven. Our parents were—" I stop, my stomach lurching at the memories crowding in. "Our parents died, and Rafe sort of took on the role of father to me. He was just fifteen."

"Lance." Charlie's voice is soft, pulling me back from the darkness. "I'm so sorry."

I turn to look her full in the face, drinking in her visage. Her loveliness, her glow, her scent all soothe me. I shake my head. "It was a long time ago. But Rafe still thinks he's responsible for everything when it comes to me. When we were young, I would try and try to prove to him I could stand on my own two feet, that I could fight my own battles and handle myself without him looking out for me, but it never took. Eventually, I gave up and became the one with zero fucks. I mean, we can't both be tightly wound all the time. I figured one of us had better go out and live."

119

Charlie's eyes go round.

Fuck. I shouldn't have told her that part. She will think that I'm not responsible. Not worthy of being a good father to our child. I pretty much just told her I'm the pack playboy. Which has been true.

"So Rafe's Mr. Serious, and you're Mr. Laid back?" Her voice is soft with understanding. I don't hear any judgement in it.

I shrug. "Yeah, I guess so. So he's busy out there thinking he needs to worry about our pup now, like I'm not a grown wolf capable of protecting my own young." I wave a hand in the direction of Rafe's bedroom.

"Yeah, I didn't like his implication," Charlie says.

"Fuck, I'm so sorry he offended you. I will make damn sure he makes it up to you."

Charlie shakes her head. "I wasn't offended. I mean, I was just offended *for you*. I felt like he was selling you short."

For a moment, I can't hear anything over the thundering in my heart. Since the day our parents died, Rafe has sown the belief that I can't take care of my own shit. No one has ever disputed that supposed fact.

"I don't think it's true that you give zero fucks. I think you've just perfected the art of being laid back. Something I'm hoping will rub off on me a little more." She flashes me a sheepish smile.

"Yeah?" I take both her hands in mine, facing her like we're standing at the altar.

"Definitely. You already know I tend to be a worrier. You might be the balance I need."

I can't wait another second. I drop her hands so I can catch her behind the head and draw her mouth to mine. I claim her with a hungry kiss. "Angel, I'm happy to be your stress relief. Any time, anywhere."

Her eyes crinkle as she smiles up at me. "Bring it," she murmurs, and it's on.

I hook my forearm under her ass and carry her to my bed, kissing the hell out of her mouth as I go. "You're about to get yourself fucked long and hard," I warn her.

Her laugh is husky. "Just so long as you don't bite." She holds a finger up between us. I pretend to snap my teeth at it and she shrieks a little, her laugh turning to a giggle.

I flip her over to her belly and deliver a slap to her sexy ass.

"Ooh." She looks over her shoulder. "Yes, please."

I chuckle, kicking off my boots and stripping out of my shirt. "I know you like to plan, angel, so here's how it's going to go." I deliver another slap before I roll her back over to get her jeans open. "I'm going to use my tongue to get you off at the same time as I spank that ass red." I tug her jeans and panties down at the same time as she toes off her shoes. "Then I'm going to stuff you full of this wolf-cock until you're screaming for release." I help her out of her shirt and bra. "And then I'm going to wrap you up in my arms and make sure nothing disturbs your sweet slumber, not even the morning sun." As soon as I have her naked, I flip her back over to her belly, and lift her hips until she's on her knees. "Got it?"

"Sounds like a good plan to me."

"Spread those knees wider."

She gives a sexy moan as she lets her knees slide open on the bed, lifting and spreading her ass toward me. I grip her cheeks to lift and separate them, opening her up for my tongue. I let the first slap on her bare skin fall at the same moment that my tongue slides between her folds.

She cries out, her legs jerking a little before she arches to give me more.

"That's right, my little planner. Let me lick what's mine."

There's a little *uhn* of protest, like she wants to dispute the fact that she's mine now, so I give her ass three spanks to prove it. Her breath shudders in, shaky and desperate. I lap at her juices, which are flowing freely now, pressing my tongue between her folds, penetrating her with it. Every few seconds, I slap her ass, keeping her on edge and gasping.

I find her clit—it's tough from this angle, but I'm dedicated—and roll my tongue around it, then deliver another spank, this time on her other cheek. I suck her labia into my mouth, nip it. I pull back and spank her pussy a few times, then pepper her ass with short, swift spanks.

"Lance," she whimpers, sounding needy.

"That's right, angel. I want you saying my name while I treat you right." I press the pad of my thumb over her anus as I return my mouth to her core.

"Oh my God, Lance."

Another slap.

"Please," she whimpers. "It's so good. Oh my God, please."

"You need to come, angel?"

"Yes!"

"Come on my tongue, Charlie, and then I'll give you my cock." I massage her anus and penetrate her with my tongue.

She reaches back with her fingers to rub her clit more firmly. I slap her ass once. Twice. On the third time, she comes, her sweet pussy clenching and shivering around my tongue as she pushes her hips back to get more of it.

"That's it, angel." I sink two fingers into her channel to give here something more substantial to clench around.

"Oh... oh! Lance."

"Yep. Only Lance," I tell her, gently tackling her to her side and pushing her onto her back.

Charlie

Lance hovers over me, staring down with glowing eyes—the palest blue.

"Your wolf is showing," I whisper.

He blinks, touching the tip of his tongue to one of his canine teeth, which appears longer than usual. "I won't mark you," he promises.

I wasn't even thinking about what he'd told me on the way over here. That his wolf wants to bite me to embed his scent forever in me. But the way he's talking, I'm getting the possessive vibe all over the place.

And I have to say... I don't hate it.

I mean, it's the last thing I'd have expected from a player like Lance. The whole reason I rejected him was because I figured he was a fly-by-night kind of guy. But now everything's changed. He says he's in it for life. He's calling my pussy his.

It hits the buttons for me. Buttons I didn't even know I had. I wanted safe, stable, and secure in a man.

I'm still not sure he's that, but he certainly is all in with me. I can't really demand more than that. He can't change who or what he is, what he does for a living, but he's willing to give me one hundred percent.

And he's five hundred times more exciting than my fantasy accountant.

And the sex.

Dear Lord.

He rubs the head of his cock over my entrance, making me arch and moan for more, even though I just came.

"Yes," I encourage.

"Say my name again." His voice is low and growly. He's withholding his cock, teasing me now.

"Lance," I answer immediately.

"Only Lance," he corrects.

"Only Lance," I agree.

His smile is feral. He shoves in with a practiced snap of his hips, and the sensation of being filled by him makes my eyes roll back in my head.

"Oh…" I moan in pleasure as he eases back, then punches in again.

"Uh-huh. You want it deep?"

"Yes," I agree. Not that I'd complain if he gave it any other way. I mean, the guy pretty much has a magic dick. Everything he does with it makes me scream.

I watch him in the moonlit room, his six-pack abs flexing as he undulates his hips, his pecs standing out in stark relief.

He braces my shoulder with one hand, tracing his thumb lightly across my throat—a gentle movement that's totally in contrast to his deep, firm thrusts. There's a meditative quality to his movements, almost like tantra—not that I know that much about it. But this is how I imagine tantric sex would be.

Maybe he's concentrating to keep himself from marking me. The thought should sober me, but it doesn't. It's hard to be afraid of anything when I'm with Lance. I meant what I told him before sex—he does balance me out. He eases my anxiety. Makes me feel like anything is possible. Like my world isn't quite so small as I try to make it. That I can let go of control, and he'll make sure nothing terrible happens.

I surrender to the delicious sweetness of him moving

inside me and roll my hips to match his thrusts, receiving him.

He cups my breast, brushing his thumb over my tightened nipple, pinching and squeezing it.

The relaxation of my first orgasm floats away, replaced by the winding coil of need. I start to whimper and moan. I grip Lance's arms, my nails sinking into his skin.

He lets loose that wicked smile again. "You want more, Charlie?"

"Yes," I beg.

He picks up his pace, shortening his thrusts to make them quick and hard. The sound of flesh slapping flesh fills the room.

"Lance…"

"Uh-huh. Say my name, Charlie. Who makes you scream?"

"You do. Oh God, please, Lance."

His eyes glow in the darkness and he stares down at me steadily, keeping up the fast pace, but not losing control himself. He seems to be waiting for me. It's all for me.

"Are you going to—" I pant.

His smile widens. "It's a given with you, angel. I'm just trying to hold back."

"Don't," I murmur.

"Fuck." Lance seems to lose control, then, slamming in with rough, jerky strokes until he thrusts deep, and stays.

I come the moment he does, my pussy milking his cum. Even though we've already conceived a child, I imagine this to be the moment we make the baby, picturing the perfection of our coupling—how my body receives his essence, welcomes it. Pulls it deeper inside me to fertilize my egg.

It's a beautiful act, creation.

What we made together is beautiful, whether we intended it at the time or not.

True to his word, Lance lowers himself onto me, wraps me in his arms, and rolls us to the side so I'm cradled against him.

The words *I love you* swim into my head. It's too soon to say them, but they're there, nonetheless. What I feel in this moment for Lance is definitely love.

I kiss his throat, his chest. He makes an almost wounded sound, and strokes my hair.

I pull back. "Are you okay? Was it hard not to mark me?"

His smile is slightly pained. "It's hard." His cock stirs against my belly, and he winks. "I'm always hard for you, though."

"Ha ha." I touch his face. "But really—does it hurt?"

He shakes his head. "No, angel. I'm just afraid I'll hurt you. I don't want to lose control and mark you without your consent. It's more of a frenzy, not a pain."

I nod and snuggle closer to him. As weird as all this is, I'm loving being a part of it. Learning about his kind. His pack. His wounds.

"How about you?" He brushes some hair back from my face. "You relaxed? Need anything?"

"I'm good. Definitely relaxed. You help me with that. I feel like I can let go of control a little bit when I'm with you. And have fun."

"Mmm. My little planner. We do have fun." He kisses my head. "Where did that need to plan and prepare come from?"

It's funny, my friends have ribbed and teased me about it for years, but no one's really asked why I'm a control freak. It's just been accepted that this is who I am.

I draw in a breath. "My parents both enlisted in the Air Force after 9/11. My childhood wasn't just moving around a lot, having my mom or dad gone for months and months. Sometimes both of them were deployed, and we stayed with my gran. Plus, I was always scared Mom or Dad wouldn't come home—because that happened to other kids I knew on base. I dreamed of my mom and dad coming home and telling us they were going to get new jobs. I just wanted them to be safe. And I wanted to live in a small town with a strong community. That's why I chose Taos. I could see myself marrying, raising kids here."

"And the man you envisioned?"

Is it just me, or does Lance's voice sound a little strangled? I swallow. "Well, honestly? I was picturing someone very stable. A dentist or an accountant." Lance wrinkles his nose at that, and I laugh. "I know, sounds boring. But mostly I was thinking someone who was grounded, who would love being a dad. Someone who would coach Little League and be a cub scout leader and all that stupid stuff."

It's funny how that all seems irrelevant now.

"I will coach *the hell* out of Little League," Lance says in the most solemnly-swearing voice.

I laugh, warmth swimming in my chest. "I bet you will."

And somehow, the thought of witnessing Lance learning to coach Little League sounds far more exciting than the picture I had in my head. The one with the boring accountant who already thought he knew everything there was to know about Little League.

I nuzzle his chest and sigh, contentment settling over me like a blanket. I can't remember when I've ever felt this at peace, but I do now. In Lance's arms, I feel safe and protected. Like everything—even an unexpected pregnancy and being mated to a werewolf—will be not only easy, but also fun.

CHAPTER 10

 ance

AFTER DROPPING Charlie at work the next morning, I find Rafe running target practice in the woods with the rest of the pack. He likes to make us train in inclement weather, and snow started falling an hour ago in thick, silent flakes.

Expecting the usual rebuke I get when I've been off having fun while the rest of them are training, I join them wordlessly, and pick up a crossbow.

I sight the target, wait, and release my arrow a second after Rafe releases his, splitting the wood shaft of his down the center as we both nail the bullseye.

"Asshole," he mutters.

I say nothing. Instead, I reload and wait.

"Are you trying to prove you don't need to train?" he snaps.

"Nope. I'm trying to prove I'm not as fucking incapable as you think I am."

"Here we go again." Rafe has the nerve to scoff.

Channing releases an arrow and I let mine fly, taking all the glory out of his bullseye when I wreck his arrow, too.

"Asshole." Channing shoots me a grin to show that, unlike Rafe, he doesn't mean it.

Despite my normally laid-back ways, I can't find it in me to smile. Hearing Charlie's perspective last night changed everything. It validated what I've felt my entire adult life, but never knew if I was just making it up.

Rafe doesn't think I can take care of myself.

"Nobody thinks you're incapable," Deke offers, sending off an arrow before I can tag onto it. He's usually the silent one, so the fact that he's trying to peace-make tells me I'm crankier than I know. My need to mark Charlie bleeds into every moment. Makes me ready to fight, fuck, or die at a moment's notice.

"Oh, really? Because I think Channing gets more respect than I do around here, and he's barely out of his training boots."

Channing whirls, aiming his arrow right at my eye. "Say that again, asshole." His goofy grin is the only thing that keeps my wolf from responding in kind.

"Oh, I'm ready." I flick my brows at him.

"Maybe because Channing isn't off knocking up humans—"

With a snarl, I leap, knocking Rafe to the ground. I'm so enraged, I don't even know if I'm in wolf form or human.

Human, it seems. With three very large other humans sitting on top of me, holding me down.

"Fates, he's got it bad," Channing crows.

"Fuck you." I struggle but can't get up. Not with all of them holding down my limbs with their entire body weight.

"You'd better mark your girl before you lose your shit," Deke says.

"Listen to me," Rafe says. "*Listen*." He infuses Alpha Command into the word, and my body instinctively goes still. "I didn't mean that. I'm sorry. I know she's your mate. But you sure as fuck did this backw—"

"I'd like to see you do things perfectly when it comes to a female," Deke growls, surprising me by taking my side and standing up to his alpha.

To my utter shock, Rafe doesn't re-establish dominance. For a second, his expression grows remote, as if he's actually thinking about a female. But that's impossible. Rafe has never been interested in seeking his alpha she-wolf mate. And it's hard to imagine he'll ever find her when we're holed up in this small town and rarely interact with other shifters.

"No," he says gruffly, suddenly getting off me. The other two follow his lead and stand. Rafe reaches a hand out to help me up.

I only take it because it's unlike him to be conciliatory.

"I just hope you're thinking about everything that could go wrong." Rafe turns away from me and rubs a palm over his closely-shorn hair, melting the snowflakes on the top of his head with his body heat.

"Why would he want to do that?" Channing asks under his breath.

"Sarcero is out there. He could be out for revenge, and how better to get it than through your female? Or through your child?"

My stomach drops.

Fuck.

I swallow, hard. "I will figure out how to keep them safe," I swear.

Rafe nods. "We all will."

I'm instantly sorry for picking a fight. I know Rafe carries the weight of the world on his shoulders. More than he should, even for an alpha of such a small pack. I step in for a bro-hug and thump his back. "I love you, man."

"Cock-sucker," Rafe mutters because he doesn't do intimacy.

Channing and I both laugh.

CHAPTER 11

 harlie

TONIGHT IS GIRLS' night and Sadie, Adele, Tabitha, and I plan
to meet at Tabitha's house. I'm going to tell them I'm expecting. Sadie already knows, and Adele knows some of my
history with Lance, but it's time to tell them all the whole
story.

Tabitha lives in a converted train car outside Taos. Her
decorating style can be summed up as: really cool clutter. It
doesn't help that half her house is dedicated to interesting
vintage objects, or clothes she sells online.

I push aside the beaded curtain and make my way to one
of the three beanbag chairs. There's a more structured modern
chaise longue-like piece of furniture available to sit in, but I
avoid it. Tabitha calls it a 'yoga couch', but I looked the
brand up online and it is definitely a sex couch. The red
pleather cover is easily wiped down, but still. Even Adele
chooses a beanbag.

Adele's already here, holding court for three dozing cats, with a fourth on her lap. In addition to her online business, Tabitha pet-sits to pay for her groceries. She's also worked as a model, an earthship builder, a jewelry artist, and an off-road Jeep racer. Career goals don't mean the same thing to Tabitha as they do to me.

She definitely doesn't have a life plan.

"Hey lady," I greet Adele. My friend looks a bit more relaxed since I saw her last. I don't want to pry into her business woes unless she brings them up first, so I settle for, "How are you doing?"

"Great." Adele strokes the giant tabby. "Getting some purr therapy."

"Oh, is Winston Churchill bothering you?" Tabitha calls from the kitchen.

"Not at all," Adele murmurs. The cat purrs so loud, I can hear him from my seat. "Charlie just got in."

"Charlie, welcome," Tabitha calls. "Make yourself at home. Anything to drink? Adele's got wine."

"Just water for me, thanks." I hold out my hand and coax one of the Siamese over.

Tabitha swings in with a bag of chips and bowl of salsa. She shoos the second Siamese cat away from the low coffee table, then props her hands on her hips. She is in a bright yellow jumpsuit, looking like Uma Thurman in *Kill Bill*. She does cosplay a lot, as well as buys vintage clothes in bulk at estate sales and uses her own sewing skills to reinvent them. The jumpsuit is probably a result of this.

"How the heck are you, Charlie?" Tabitha asks, still bustling around, setting out coasters and rearranging the snacks. "I haven't seen you around."

Probably because I've been shacking up with Lance instead of helping Adele at the shop. The guy spent every night this week making sure I'm thoroughly and well-satisfied sexually both before bed, and every morning before work. And the rest of his hours are spent offering me food, or showing up in wolf form on my mail route. "I'm good."

"You look great. Are you wearing makeup or something?" Tabitha peers at me. "You're glowing."

"Yes, you are," Adele agrees, and arches a brow at me behind Tabitha's back.

I touch my cheeks, hoping the low light from the lava lamp hides my blush. Fortunately, Tabitha doesn't pry. She dips a chip and takes it to the yoga/sex couch, where she sprawls out on the curved surface. "Oh, before I forget, Adele, I saw your business partner the other day. He looked like he had a black eye."

I shoot a worried glance at Adele. Bing didn't have a black eye when I saw him, but she doesn't look surprised by the news.

"Oh?" Adele's voice is neutral.

"I called his name but he must not have heard me." Tabitha shrugs. "Everything okay?"

"Yeah, I called him earlier, but haven't heard back from him," Adele says slowly. "Thanks for the update, Tabitha. I'll see if he calls back."

"No problem." Tabitha seems oblivious, so Adele must not have shared everything with her yet. "Charlie? What's new with you?"

"Um…" Should I catch them up now, or wait for Sadie? I can't decide. My pause goes on for too long, and I realize my two friends are staring at me expectantly. "I do have some news."

Adele hides her smile in her wine glass. She thinks she knows what I'm going to say.

I open my mouth, and the door swings open.

"Hey ladies," Sadie trills. "You ready to be godmothers?" She's carrying a big Tupperware container—the one she uses for baked goods—and a bag full of clinking bottles. "I figured we can celebrate. I made cupcakes! And brought stuff for mocktails!"

Adele straightens so fast, Winston Churchill the cat goes flying. He lands on his feet with a thump and struts away, tail in the air. Adele doesn't notice. "Godmothers?" She eyes Sadie as if looking for a baby bump.

"Mocktails? Tabitha wrinkles her nose. She turns to me. "Is that your news? Are you detoxing?"

"Oh no," Sadie gasps. I grab the plastic container of cupcakes before they go flying, too, and get them safely to the coffee table. "You haven't told them yet?" Sadie's aghast.

Adele's hazel eyes widen as they switch from Sadie to me. "Charlie?"

"Surprise,'" I say weakly to Tabitha and Adele.

Adele puts a hand to her mouth.

"Wait, what?" Tabitha asks, looking from my face to Adele's. "What's going on?"

I clear my throat. "I'm pregnant."

"Congratulations," Sadie bursts out, just like the first time I told her. "Sorry. I'm just so excited."

"Oh my God, really?" Tabitha asks. I nod, and she pumps her fist in the air. "Rizzo's got a bun in the oven!"

Oh my God.

"Charlie, are you okay?" Adele asks.

"Yes?" I answer. "I mean, I'm getting there. It's still a shock."

"It'll be okay." Sadie sinks into a beanbag next to me. "That's what we're here for." She pats my knee.

Tabitha makes a beeline for the cupcakes which Sadie made with pale blue, pink, and yellow frosting.

"Yes," Adele says. "We're here for you. Whatever you need…"

I wilt a little, weak with relief.

"Wait, I didn't even know you were seeing anyone." Tabitha licks blue frosting off her finger.

"I wasn't." Gah, I have to catch Tabitha up on everything.

"So what happened? Who's the lucky guy?" She grins and adds mischievously, "Do you know?"

"Stop." Adele frowns at Tabitha.

Tabitha winks at me.

"Yes, I know the guy," I snark back. Tabitha and I like to pretend-fight. "It's Lance Lightfoot."

Tabitha pauses before biting into a cupcake. "Wait, who?"

"One of those bikers," Adele says.

"Deke's friend," Sadie puts in quickly.

I can't read Adele's expression. I'm not sure she's going to approve of Lance.

Tabitha's mouth falls open. "The blond playboy? That's your baby-daddy?"

"Yes, and we really hit it off. We're going to try to make it work."

"Yay" Sadie claps her hands and starts pulling bottles of fancy seltzers and syrups from her bag.

Adele looks skeptical.

Tabitha comes over and sets a cupcake in front of me. "Back the baby-mobile up a second," she says. "I feel like I'm missing a lot. Let me get this straight: you are with Lance? The guy who hit on an entire cluster of coed ski-bunnies in front of us?"

I wince. We had watched Lance do that. And all of the girls had given him their numbers. One squeezed his muscles and asked if she could ride his bike. He assured them all he'd take them for a long, hard ride.

I groan and put my face in my hands. Immediately, my friends surround me. Three gentle hands fall on my back. Even Tabitha is here for me.

"It's okay," Adele says. "We've got you."

"Yeah, Charlie," Tabitha adds and Sadie finishes, "We're going to get through this."

"I know he's a player. It was just a birthday indulgence. He bought me a drink after we celebrated my birthday—we met in the parking lot. Actually, we met at the hot springs that morning—naked. And that set the stage." I can't resist a naughty grin that makes my friends *ooh* and laugh.

"So," Tabitha says, "he must be good."

"Really good," I admit with a sigh. "So very good."

"But?" Adele prompts, hearing my reluctance. She holds out the plate of cupcakes, and I take one.

"But I wanted someone stable. A homebody like me. Lance isn't in the military anymore, but I think his job is just as dangerous—or even more so now than when he was." I peel back the wrapper of the cupcake and take a bite. It's perfect: moist and spongy with just the right amount of icing. The sugary sweetness melts on my tongue.

Sadie sobers. "I worry about that, too," she admits, unwrapping her own cupcake. "But they're strong guys." She gives me a meaningful look. I know I'm not allowed to tell Tabitha and Adele about the pack—what they are. I don't know how Sadie could stand it when none of us knew. At least now we can talk to each other.

I mix myself a mocktail. Adele and Tabitha spike theirs to make the real thing. "They are... but it's still dangerous business." I can't stop thinking about those bullet holes in Lance. Last night, I had a nightmare that I was up at night to feed the baby, and found Lance bleeding out on my kitchen floor.

"But it does seem pretty lucrative," Tabitha offers. "I

mean, those guys bought that multimillion dollar property on the way to the ski valley for their headquarters. They must be doing well."

I nod. "Yes, I think you're right. Which reinforces my belief that it's highly dangerous. Maybe not even legal."

"It's legal," Sadie says staunchly. "Or at least it's at the behest of the U.S. government."

"Not necessarily the same thing," I counter.

Sadie's brow creases with worry, and I kick myself for transferring my anxieties to her. If she's blissfully happy with her new wolf-mate, I shouldn't poop on her party.

"So he's all in with the pregnancy? I mean, what did he say?" Tabitha asks.

I take a long swig of my mocktail. "Yeah. He's all in. He's at my place every night, making sure I've eaten, and rubbing my feet. It's pretty unbelievable, really."

"So do you believe him?" Adele asks. She doesn't sound judgmental; just like she's trying to get the facts straight. "Is he for real?"

If it weren't for the wolf part, I wouldn't believe any of it. But this guy isn't human. So that means I can't pigeon-hole him into the box where I thought he belonged. "Yes, I think he is. And he's not what I would've picked—far from it—but we have enough chemistry that I want to give it a try."

"All right," Tabitha says. I know she'll support me. And if Lance does ever cheat on me, she'll be the first one to egg his house, send glitter bombs to his place of work, and put sugar in his Duke's gas tank.

"What about baby names?" Sadie says. "Have you thought of any?"

I brighten. "Actually, I have."

"Right." Tabitha rolls her eyes. "Your perfect life plan." She puts *life plan* in air quotes.

"Behave," Adele cautions.

"It's not like her life plan is written down in a big binder with tabs color-coded by decade," Sadie scoffs.

There's a silence as my three friends look at me.

"It's not color-coded," I mumble. "That's a good idea."

Tabitha snorts.

"What?" I throw up my hands. "I like to have all my goals in one place."

"And there's nothing wrong with that," Adele says.

"Well, if you need help with baby names, I've got a few." Tabitha pours some blackberry syrup into her cup, takes a sip, and smacks her lips.

"Oh do you now?" I cross my arms over my chest.

"Here we go," Adele mutters.

"Gorgon," Tabitha says with a straight face. "Good strong name."

"What? No!" Sadie cries.

"Scheherazade. Another great one. Strong woman. Boudicca. Another strong warrior woman."

"I like old-fashioned names," I cut Tabitha off before she really gets going, but I'm grinning. "Like Opal and Jonas."

"Boudicca is a good old-fashioned name," Tabitha argues. "Or what about something Biblical? Like Rahab or Belshazzar."

"Nebuchadnezzar," Adele mutters.

"Yes." Tabitha points at Adele. "Exactly. Nickname *Nebu* or *Nezzar*."

"You're not serious, Tabitha," Sadie says, sounding unsure.

"I think Nebuchadnezzar is a great name," Tabitha says, all innocent. I glare at her, and she grins into her glass.

"Actually, I was thinking of going with 'J' names," I say sweetly.

"Oh lordy," Adele says. "I went to school with a family. Every kid of theirs had a 'J' name. From Joshua to Jordan to Josiah. Thank goodness they stopped after eight kids; they'd run out of names."

"Jael and Jehoshaphat," Tabitha offers.

"Jafar and Jasmine," I whip back.

"Yes," Tabitha shouts over Sadie's laughter. "Do it, Charlie. I dare you."

"If you name that child Nebuchadnezzar," Adele starts, and I hold up a hand.

"I won't, I promise." My cheeks hurt from smiling.

"Then I think you'll be fine," Adele says.

"Oh, yeah, Charlie, you've got this," Tabitha says.

"Let us know if you have any cravings, and we'll help you out," Sadie adds. "I'm in the mood to bake things."

"And if you're craving something delicious, we'll help you eat," Tabitha says. "But not if it's gross—like pretzels dipped in pickle juice."

I stick my tongue out at Tabitha. She makes the face back at me, and then we both smile. I feel a lot better. My friends are awesome, and they'll help. Even if my life's in a snarl and I don't feel ready yet to be a mother, my kid will have the best three godmothers on the face of the Earth.

harlie

SATURDAY MORNING, Lance tells me he wants to help me relax for the weekend. He corrals me into his brother's Humvee. "Come on," he says, "I have a surprise for you."

Surprise. I sort of hate surprises. I mean, how do you plan properly?

But it's Lance, who makes me feel like I'd be safe anywhere, who I trust to take care of all my needs, because he's made it his life's mission.

"We're flying somewhere?" I ask, digging my nails into my jeans so I don't bite them off.

"Maybe."

Lance drives down the road toward the tiny Taos airport. The not knowing drives me nuts. Meanwhile, Lance sits completely relaxed, one big hand on the steering wheel, the other one covering my knee. Maybe some of his calm will rub off on me.

He passes the terminal and drives us to a smaller building near the runway. A bunch of small white planes sit, waiting for their flights.

"We're taking a private flight?" I ask.

"That's right, baby. Nothing but the best. But it's a military plane so it's a little stripped to the bare bones. Come on." He gets out and gets my door.

I grab my purse. "Um, did I need to bring anything?"

"Nope, just you." He kisses me and takes my hand, a giant grin on his face. Like a little boy who is going to show me his toys. His grown-up and very expensive toys.

Our plane is the last one on the tarmac, a boxy-looking one painted a dull grey-green. Army green. It's pretty bare inside, with an open cockpit and a few simple hard seats folded up between hanging straps.

I have a thought. "Lance," I say nervously, "we're not going skydiving?"

"Nah, angel. Nothing like that. This weekend is all about you and me relaxing together." He leads me to the middle of the seating area, where two comfier looking seats have been retrofitted in between the basic ones.

"So where are we going?" I clutch my purse, wondering how in the hell Lance managed to get me here without giving me any details. I feel naked, being in a plane without a suitcase. I at least would have packed a carry-on bag with some essentials.

"You'll see."

He kisses my forehead then drops his head to brush his mouth against mine. I lean into him and the kiss, then give a start as the doors begin to close. Someone's climbed into the cockpit.

"All right, this is it." Lance buckles me in. "Strap you in, nice and tight."

Another kiss, and the plane engines start to roar.

"Might be a little louder than you're used to," Lance shouts over the noise. But his excitement is catching, and my heart is pumping after that kiss. Lance straps himself in right next to me and settles his hand over my knee. I lean back with a smile. Maybe this could be fun.

"So what do you say?" hollers the pilot. "Wanna do some barrel rolls?"

"Nothing but the easiest ride for my girl," Lance calls back.

"Is that Teddy?" I point to the front. Sadie told me about him, and the epic helicopter ride Deke took her on for a date.

"That's my name," the pilot hollers back. Somehow he heard me over the noise. "Coz I'm cuddly like a teddy bear."

I crane my head around Lance. Teddy is a giant dude in a cut off shirt that shows off his tattoo-covered arms, bulging with muscles. He's definitely not soft and squishy like a stuffed toy. His muscles have muscles.

"Don't flirt with my mate," Lance shouts back. His body's still relaxed but there's a whisper of a threat behind his words.

"Is he a wolf shifter, too?" I guess, since Lance used the word *mate* with him.

"Bear, baby," Teddy calls, again hearing me when I don't think it should be possible.

"Call her baby again," Lance grits out, "and I'll castrate you."

"Who's doing the favors here?" Teddy pokes back.

"Doesn't mean you can cross any lines."

Teddy grins over his shoulder. "Take it easy. I'm just giving you a hard time." He sends me another wink.

I relax. I can trust these guys, even if I don't know the

plan. Between the noise and my new pregnancy tiredness, I doze for the rest of the flight.

I wake a few hours later when the plane touches down on a small runway. "Hey, angel, we're here." Lance lifts my hand and kisses my knuckles. As we exit, I wave to Teddy. He gives me a two-finger salute.

"Take it easy, baby-mama," he says, aviator shades flashing over his grin. He grins bigger when Lance growls.

We step out of the plane, and warm air hits my face. I tilt my head to the sun. "Where are we?"

I was supposed to watch the landscape and guess, but there weren't any windows. Plus, I fell asleep.

"I figured a day at the beach would be nice." He shrugs. "You work too hard. You need to relax and soak up some sun. Come on. I got them to leave us a car."

We're definitely somewhere warm. A few palm trees dot the desert landscape, and a few mountains slope along the horizon.

We walk over the tarmac, bypassing the tiny building that passes for a terminal, and heading for the parking lot. This is as small an airport as the one we left, and that's saying something. "Who's *they*?"

"Our friends. I called in a favor." He takes my arm and my purse and guides me to a big black Escalade. He punches in a code on a keypad on the door, and it unlocks. In a minute, we're passing a big sign that reads: 'Welcome to Cabo San Lucas'.

"Oh my gosh," I cry. "We're in Cabo? Just like that?"

"Just like that," he confirms. He reaches across to the glove box, pulls out a pair of aviator sunglasses, and puts them on. He hands a second pair to me.

"What about passports? And customs?"

"I called in some favors. We're fine. It can be easy, Charlie. Life can be like this." He drives one handed again so his right hand can massage the back of my neck briefly. "Just take it easy."

The windows are down and when we wind over the mountain rise, I get a whiff of salt air. *Relax, Charlie. It's a day at the beach.* Blue ocean, bright sun and ice cream. Even I can't get stressed about this.

We pass through the resort town. I keep expecting Lance to turn into one of the hotels, but we zoom by and turn into a private road. There's a gate ahead. Lance stops to punch in a code and wave to the camera. The gates open and we glide on through.

"Who exactly are your friends?" I ask. The houses in this gated community aren't houses. These are mansions, set on the side of the mountain overlooking the ocean.

"They're shifters. We tend to get to know each other. We helped them out with security from time to time, so it wasn't a big deal to call in a favor."

Great. Millionaire shifters. Maybe I should have dressed up. At the very least, I shouldn't have worn my Sasquatch 'Hide'n Seek World Champion' t-shirt.

We turn into a private drive paved with stone, lined with palm trees and cacti. The house is built on a bluff over the harbor. It's sprawling, several stories, with a multi-colored adobe roof and stucco in different shades of sunset colors.

"This is huge," I say. "Is it a hotel?"

"Nope, private residence. Ten bedrooms, I think. Infinity pool." He parks and I half expect armed security to rush up to the car and escort us off the premises. "What do you think, babe? Will this be suitable?"

"Oh my God," I mumble.

He strides up to the house with perfect confidence.

Another keyless entry. The door opens without a sound, and I cling to his hand as I shuffle over the marble floors.

"Is anyone home?" I whisper. If I lived here I'd never leave.

"Just us."

We enter a huge room that faces the ocean. Panoramic views all around. There's a huge patio with hammocks strung between the marble columns. We can sit and watch the sunsets here.

Lance points out the fire pit and grill area. The infinity pool is built to look like it's floating in the ocean.

I wander to find a bathroom and return shaking my head. "The master suite is larger than my house."

"They're all that big, angel." Lance has already raided the fridge. He hands me a water bottle before swigging from his. "And then there are two guest houses."

I clutch my water. Did I really just walk into a rich person's home and help myself to their water? "This is incredible. And you know people who live here?"

"They don't live here. This is just one of their homes."

I rub my forehead. A noise makes me turn. There's a huge TV on the far wall, behind a bar-height table and stools. A *Cheers* style bar, recreated inside someone's house. Light flickers on the screen as the TV comes to life—a screen bigger than my dining room table.

Pinkish shadows, and then a little face backs away from the camera. It's an adorable little girl with a white bow askew in her brown hair. She's in a yellow dress with what looks like purple paint smeared on the front.

"Hello." She waves.

I wave back, unsure if she can see me.

"Jaylin," someone calls off screen. "Jaylin, are you done with the paint? Oh, damn it." A brunette comes into view.

"Dammit," the little girl echoes.

"No, Jaylin. What did Mommy say about swearing?" The woman crouches down to dab a wet cloth at the purple smears on the girl's dress.

"Don't do it in front of anybody," Jaylin answers dutifully.

"That's right," the mother says. "They might judge me."

I must have made a noise because the mom raises her head. "Oh wait, did you turn on the screen? Is that…" The woman peers at the screen and waves. "Hi, there."

"Hello." I guess she can see me.

"I'm Kylie. I left the CallBot out because I was going to check on you guys later. I guess Jaylin got it to dial you. She uses this all the time to call her great-grandma upstairs. Anyway, did you get in okay?"

"Got in just fine," Lance calls from across the room. He bounds up to my side and puts his arm around me. "Thanks so much."

"Oh, no problem. We'll be down there in a few days, so it should be stocked with everything you need."

"Awesome, thanks," Lance says. "Kylie, this is my mate, Charlie." He squeezes me tighter.

"Hello." I wave. Then I realize Lance called me *mate*.

"Is this…"

"Yep, they own the place."

"My beach house," Jaylin says. Kylie laughs and draws her daughter onto her lap. "That's right, Jaylin, all yours." She rolls her eyes.

"We go there in my white plane," Jaylin explains proudly, her little voice adorably squeaky.

"Yes," Kylie says, "we'll go there in our white plane in a few days."

"What color is your plane?" Jaylin asks.

"Green," I answer.

"That's nice." She twists to face her mother. "Can I have a green plane?"

"I think one plane is enough," Kylie says and kisses the top of her daughter's head. "Now go play."

"Okay." Jaylin pushes off her mother's lap and waves to me with a small hand. "Bye."

"Bye." My hand goes to my belly. I'm surprisingly choked up seeing a mom and daughter. One day, the baby in my belly will be this big and this adorable.

"Charlie is, ah, new to our kind," Lance says. "She's carrying my pup."

"Oh, yes." Kylie cocks her head at me. She's as beautiful as her daughter. "I'm half-shifter, like your pup will be, but I didn't know what I was until I met my mate. Get my number from Lance. You can always call if you have questions."

"Thanks." I clear my throat. I'm not going to get choked up by this woman's generosity. "I will."

"Wow," I say to Lance when Kylie ends the call.

"I know, right? She and Jackson are pretty cool. Well, Jackson's a little stiff, but Kylie has softened him. She's not a wolf—she's some kind of cat. Panther, I think. Or maybe jaguar. Her shifter genes didn't kick in until she got pregnant. There's lots of shifters like that we know. We can meet them, if you want."

I stroke my belly. I want my kid to know his or her people. "I think I'd like that."

"But enough about that. Today's about fun. You wanna take a swim?"

"Definitely. But…" I look around as if expecting a bikini to appear magically. "Aren't you forgetting something? I didn't bring a bag." He could have at least told me to pack a swimsuit. Ridiculous man.

"No problem." Lance slants me a grin and slowly strips off his shirt. I'd pay good money for a striptease like this. Lust pushes the thoughts out of my head for a moment.

His hands go to his jeans. He holds my gaze as he undoes the top button and draws down the zipper.

Is it getting hot in here?

He kicks off his shoes, and I realize what he's planning. "You're not going to…"

He just gives me a grin.

"Lance, no." I cross my arms over my chest. "We can't skinny dip. Not here." Some rich person will see us and swoon into their caviar, clutching their South Sea pearls.

"No one will see us. Charlie, relax."

This man. He's going to drive me to drink. Except I can't drink for the next nine months.

"Race ya. Last one in gets dunked." He winks, and it's on.

I strip.

~

Lance

I let Charlie win, of course. No way I'd ever dunk my female. Or let her lose anything but her heart. And, of course, her clothes.

The water in the pool is warm, and Charlie cuts through the water like an Olympic swimmer.

"That's an impressive freestyle you have there," I say when she finally swims up to me, a smile lighting up her face.

"I won first place at State in high school."

I slide my hands down her sides. "So many things I don't know about you yet. I want to learn them all."

Her lids droop. "Is this really how it's going to be? All the time?"

I stop stroking. "What do you mean?"

"Is this our honeymoon phase? And then you turn into a lazy, bossy jerk with a beer gut who lies on the couch and doesn't take out the garbage?"

I laugh so loud, I startle her. "Is that what you're worried about today, angel?"

She blushes. "Not really. I just don't want to get used to you being so into me if one day it's going to stop."

I hold her gaze. "I told you, it never stops. Not until the day I die, angel. Wolves mate for life. We don't fuck around. And," I take her hand and bring it to my washboard abs, "luckily for you, we don't often get beer guts."

Her smile grows sultry as she runs both palms over my abs. "That *is* lucky," she murmurs. Then her smile fades. "But my body won't be so perfect. Especially not after a pregnancy."

I cup both her breasts and back her against the pool wall. "What do I have to do to make you believe me? I will always be hot for you. It's biological. Nothing will change my need to satisfy you. To take care of you." I slide one hand down her belly and cup between her legs.

She lets out a soft moan. I drop down under the water to push her legs open and use my tongue. I hear her muffled scream and her legs thrash around my shoulders. She taps on my head. I ignore her, sucking her nether lips, nipping, trying to get her swollen clit between my lips. She taps more insistently.

I resurface, grinning.

"Don't make me worry about you drowning." She slaps my chest with a wet palm.

I laugh and scoop her into my arms, carrying her to the pool steps. "I guess I'll just have to take you out of the pool to ravish you," I tell her.

"Mmm," she agrees as I climb the steps and carry her out of the pool. "I think you should always use the word *ravish* when you're talking about your intentions with me." She looks down at me and her breath catches. "Your wolf is showing."

I'm sure she's right. My wolf leaps to the surface every time I'm near her, especially when she's naked. "I won't hurt you," I promise, laying her gently on a chaise-longue.

"Maybe you should," she offers in barely more than a whisper.

I go still, my teeth punching out of my gums, my cock lurching painfully in her direction. I work hard to school my breath. I've been half-crazed all week, my wolf in a frenzy to mark her, but I've worked hard not to let it show.

Still, if I don't mark her soon, I could do it by accident, after losing control. It could go badly.

"I'll be careful," I promise. "I won't go deep."

Charlie's gaze holds trepidation, but I see excitement there, too, and the scent of her arousal wafts around me like a sweet perfume. "Okay," she says softly.

"Where do you want it? Somewhere no one will see?" I brush the backs of my fingers between her breasts, down her soft belly.

She rolls to her side and strokes her own ass. "How about here?"

"Aw, Fates, angel. That's hot. Really hot." I hook her top leg over my arm to spread her knees, and go to town with my tongue between her legs. It's so much better out of the pool where I can taste her tangy essence, feel her every tremble. I trace inside her labia, push my tongue into her entrance. I eat her ass, making her squeal and squirm.

Normally, a mating bite would happen at the height of an orgasm. My wolf would take over, my teeth would grow, coated with a special serum embedded with my scent, and I'd sink them into her flesh at the moment we both reached ecstasy. But that doesn't feel safe. Not with a human mate. Especially not a pregnant human mate. I slide a finger into Charlie, knowing her moan of pleasure will bring my wolf out. It definitely makes my dick punch out hard. I screw a second finger in and caress her inner wall, looking for her G-spot.

Her moans get louder and needier. I flick my tongue over her clit. My wolf roars to the surface. I withdraw my fingers from Charlie and close her knees, finding her anus with my thumb at the same moment I sink my fangs into her beautiful ass.

She cries out in pain, which immediately subdues my wolf. Carefully, very carefully, I withdraw my fangs from her sweet flesh and lick the wounds to aid their healing. All the time, I massage her back hole to keep the sensations erotic.

"Angel, are you all right? Please talk to me."

"Is it over?" she asks breathlessly, like the kid who looks away while getting a shot.

"Yeah. I'm so sorry it hurt." I kiss all around the puncture wounds, my other thumb sliding between her legs to rub her clit.

She shakes her head. "It doesn't hurt. I mean, it hurt a little, but I'm okay." She peers at me from under the blonde strands of hair cascading in her face. "Please say you're going to finish."

Fates know I want to finish. But I don't want to cause Charlie any pain. "Come here." I lift her up off the chaise and sit down on it, then pull her to straddle me, lying back. "You ride, angel. I don't want to hurt you any more."

Charlie's lids droop as she climbs on top of me, then lines

the head of my cock up with her entrance and seats herself. "I get to drive?" she asks in a husky voice.

"You can drive any time you want to, angel. I'm only bossy when you want me to be."

She rocks her hips over mine, sending me into spasms of ecstasy. "I do like it when you're bossy." Her voice is practically a purr. "I could even get used to your surprises," she admits.

I would answer, but I'm already halfway to the moon.

"Your wolf is happy," she murmurs.

I grip her waist and thrust up into her. "How can you tell?"

"I don't know." She rides me harder, making it difficult to concentrate on her words. "I just can tell."

"I'm so fucking happy, Charlie. You just made me the happiest guy in the world."

She draws in a sharp breath and her hands drop to my shoulders. She glides her slick pussy up and down over my rigid cock, grinding her clit down against my loins, taking me deep inside her with each forward thrust. She starts sounding off with the sexiest little cries in the galaxy, and then we both come in perfect concert. I grip her hips and pull her down snug, and she squeezes my dick in rapid pulses with her internal muscles, milking my cock for every last drop of cum.

Charlie drops down on top of me, her hard nipples coasting through my chest hair. I cradle the back of her head and hold her.

"So, is this the equivalent of marriage? We just sealed the deal?" she asks teasingly when she lifts her head.

"Yep. I'm forever yours now, angel. And you will never, ever be rid of me."

"Hmm, super-hot wolf guy whose sole purpose seems to

be to feed me, fly me to exotic beaches, and give me orgasms? I think I'm cool with that."

I caress her lips with mine. "I love you," I declare, then freeze. "Is it too soon to say that?"

"Um, you just mated me for life. So… no. Humans would usually do the love thing first."

"Where are you with it?" As soon as I ask, I'm sorry I did. I don't need to pressure her, and I'm not sure I want to hear if she's going to throw more reservations up at me.

"Falling. Hard."

"Yeah?"

"Yeah. Also, I'm afraid my butt's going to get sunburned. I think we should go inside."

Sunburn. Fuck. I scoop my laughing mate into my arms and stand in one smooth motion, then carry her inside Jackson and Kylie's mansion, where I can spend the rest of the afternoon ravishing her on a nice soft bed, away from the danger of sunburn.

harlie

CABO IS INCREDIBLE. I love Lance for bringing me here. For making me like surprises. For making it his mission to help me chill out. Release control. Stop planning and worrying.

We spend the day lounging around in the mansion, then take a sunset walk on the beach. Sunday morning, after Lance has made me scream his name several times and fed me two breakfasts, I take a walk out by the pool and call my parents.

It's time I filled them in on my enormous life change.

My mom picks up immediately, singing my name out in total joy. "Charlotte! How are you, sweetheart?" My parents retired from the Air Force last year and settled south of Tucson, where they had been stationed, in a retirement community in Green Valley. My dad now drives a golf cart around and dominates the Sunday men's bike riding group. My mom is taking painting lessons and hosting themed dinner parties.

It's ridiculously cute.

"I'm good. I'm actually in Cabo right now."

"Cabo! You didn't tell me you were taking a vacation. I'd like to know if you're leaving the country." There's a little sternness in my mother's voice. I might have gotten this worry gene from her.

I laugh. "I know, I know. Believe me, I would've told you if I'd known I was going. It was actually a surprise."

"Well, what happened? Are you all right?"

"What is it?" my dad booms in the background. "Where is she? Does she need help?"

Ah, my parents. Always ready to save me and the world.

Maybe that's one of the reasons I love Lance—there's a familiarity to this, except my parents were uptight and Lance is laid-back.

"I'm okay, totally fine. I actually have some news. Big news."

"Oh God, tell me you didn't just elope with someone? That's not like you."

I cluck my tongue. "No, it's not, so why would you even think that? Actually, I'm pregnant." Better to just get it out, right?

My mom gasps. "She's pregnant," she whisper-shouts to my dad.

"What?" my dad booms in the background.

"My, um, boyfriend surprised me with this trip to Cabo this weekend to get out of the cold and try to de-stress from the shock of it all. It obviously wasn't planned."

"No, well… that's all right," my mom says, quickly coming on board. "We're delighted for you. You're keeping it, right?"

"Of course I'm keeping it! I'm really happy. It was unexpected, but definitely not unwanted."

"And your boyfriend? You didn't even tell us you were seeing anyone."

"I know. It wasn't really serious until now, but he's great," I rush to explain. "He's retired military. He actually was able to hook me up with a call with Chad. He's still well-connected." I'm picking the things that will impress my parents, and it works.

"Wow, he must be. Where did you meet him? Does he live in Taos?"

"Yes, we met at the hot springs, actually. But his buddy is engaged to my friend Sadie, so we're already in the same circles. He's a great guy. He's going to make a great dad."

"That's great, sweetheart. So when are you due? Are you two going to get married?"

My hand drops to my ass, which is still sore from the puncture wounds, but much better than I expected. Lance said his saliva has properties that prevent infection and may speed healing. "Um, yeah, we probably will. I mean, we will. I obviously haven't had time to plan anything yet, but you'll be the first to know when I do."

"And the due date?"

"August eighth."

"Summer baby! That's great. We want to come out for the birth, of course. Will that be all right?"

My eyes mist. "I'd love that, Mom." My voice clogs. I can't believe it. I'm having a baby. The thought of having my parents sharing in the joy of the birth makes it all seem real.

And then I suddenly realize that I have no idea what a half-shifter birth will be like. Are my parents even allowed to witness it? Will the baby look normal? Oh God, so many questions.

As if Lance somehow senses my rising panic, he suddenly

appears, carrying a glass of iced lemonade and pressing it into my hand with a kiss at my temple.

"We want to meet your boyfriend, too. You didn't even say his name."

"Lance," I say, meeting his cornflower blue eyes. The ones that change to pale blue when he's a wolf. "He's great." I hold his gaze. "You're going to love him."

I hear my dad grumbling something in the background. Apparently so does Lance because he wraps an arm around me from behind and presses his lips to my ear. "Don't worry about your dad. I'll win him over."

I lean into him and say my goodbyes to my parents, then turn in his arms. "Promise me something?" I ask.

"What is it?"

"Don't show my dad your motorcycle or ever tell him that you let me drive it. Or ride on it. Okay? He's protective as hell."

Lance grins. "As he should be. Don't worry. I know his type." He points at his chest. "Retired military, remember? I may seem laid back, but I know how to play the part of serious soldier. I'll convince him I'm right for you."

I press my body against his. "It's not so much serious soldier I need, but serious dad and serious husband." I poke his chest. "Can you be very serious for me?"

Lance gives me his most laid-back grin. "I thought I was supposed to be chilling you out."

"True, but I need—"

"I know what you need." Lance loops a hand behind my back and draws me tight against him. His lips explore the side of my neck. "And I think we have time for one more quickie before we have to meet Teddy at the airstrip."

A shiver of pleasure runs through me and once more, I

loosen my grip on all my worries and let Lance carry me back into the mansion for another round.

CHAPTER 14

$\mathcal{L}$ance

Two weeks after Cabo, Charlie has her first visit at the Ob/Gyn. She had to reschedule her initial appointment because she was afraid they'd see the bite marks on her ass, which killed me, but she's healed fast—the wounds are fully closed and faded now.

She had to come during work hours, so I meet her there.

She sits on the examination table in her gown, her face drawn and pale.

"Everything will be fine, right? With the baby? There aren't weird complications because of the mixed species?"

I move to stand in front of her, my hands resting on her hips. "If anything, it's the opposite, angel," I reassure her. "Our baby will be strong. He or she won't get sick. They won't be susceptible to diseases or injuries. Even if they never shift, I think most halflings are blessed with strength and good health.

Her brows fly up. "Some don't shift?"

Damn. I'm trying to get her to relax, not freak out. "It's okay, angel. Our pups will be perfect, whether their genes manifest as human or shifter."

Her eyes grow bright. "Pups... plural?"

"Well, yeah. I mean, if you want. I definitely want more than one."

A smile tugs at her lips.

"You?" I ask.

"Yeah. I want two. A boy and a girl."

"In that order?"

"Yes. But as Adele keeps telling me: *we plan, God laughs*. That's what her grandmother used to tell her, anyway, and it seems to be true in my case."

A light tap sounds on the door and a smiling, dark-skinned female doctor comes in. She's friendly, and has a very laid-back demeanor, something I thank Fates for.

"Hi there, I'm Dr. Johnson." She shakes my hand.

"Lance Lightfoot."

"Charlie, it's good to see you again."

"Thanks," Charlie says weakly. She's already peed on a stick and had her weight measured. The nurse told us that the doctor would probably do an ultrasound today, since Charlie was worried about having taken the birth control pills for the first couple of weeks.

The doctor asks her a few questions and then asks if she wants an ultrasound. When Charlie agrees, she squirts jelly onto her belly and presses the wand against her abdomen.

The rapid tap-tap-tap of our baby's heartbeat comes through and Charlie tears up. "Sounds good to me." Dr.

Johnson smiles at Charlie. "Your baby is just about the size of a grain of rice."

I squeeze Charlie's hand and lean my head against hers. "All good, angel."

"Yes, all good. Any questions for me?" the doctor asks.

Charlie opens her mouth, then looks at me and closes it again. "I don't think so," she says weakly.

"Okay, I'd like to see you again in a month. Here's some information on recommended diet. I'll write you a prescription for prenatal vitamins, or you can buy them yourself. With your insurance, the prescription makes them a little cheaper for you."

The doctor leaves and Charlie gets dressed. As she yanks on her postal uniform, she blurts, "Oh my God, Lance, halfway through that, I suddenly started worrying that she would see something to clue her in that the baby isn't human. But you wouldn't have let me come here if there would be a problem, right?"

"You're not giving birth to a wolf, Charlie. There's nothing odd to see. Now if they want to start taking blood for tests, I'd have to stop them, but that shouldn't happen until the baby's born."

Charlie's eyes are round and wide. "But…"

I hold her shoulders. "There's nothing at all to worry about."

"How will you stop them if they want to take blood?"

I shrug. "I'd figure something out."

"Should I even have this baby with human doctors? I mean, are there shifter doctors somewhere that we should use instead?"

I rub my forehead. "Maybe. I don't know. Shifters don't get sick, so we don't need doctors. I can look into it." I seriously doubt I'd find anything, but you never know. More and more shifters seem to be mating with humans, something that has a lot of the packs alarmed for the fear that our species will die out. I hadn't paid much attention to the talk because I was in the service and never planned on mating. But now that Fate paired me with a human, I can only surmise that it's for our survival, not the other way around. Fate doesn't make mistakes.

"Maybe I should have a home-birth," Charlie says when we walk outside.

I stop and look toward the mountains, considering. "I don't know, angel. If something went wrong—not with the baby, but with you—we'd need human doctors. I want you to be safe."

"Oh."

I nudge Charlie toward her car and hold the door while she climbs in. "Everything will be fine. Nothing to worry about. I'll follow you home, okay?"

Charlie's brow furrows. "I… I think I need a little alone time. Just to process everything. Can we skip tonight?"

My heart stutters.

Fuck.

"Angel, what's bothering you? How can I help?"

"No, nothing. Don't freak out. I just need some space. This is all really fast, and I have to get used to the idea of having a wolf pup. And being your mate. And everything that goes with it. Is it fair to ask for a night off?" She says it kindly, but her words still pierce my heart.

Of course, I hold my palms out. "Of course, Charlie. Take all the time you need." I lean in and drop a kiss on her forehead. "Be sure to eat as soon as you get home."

She smiles up at me. "Cross my heart."

I wink as I close the door, but I don't feel light about the way we parted. Not at all.

Charlie's having doubts, and I don't like it one bit.

Charlie

I need a walk to clear my head. And I need to pick up the prenatal vitamins, anyway.

I'm walking up the sidewalk near Adele's shop when I notice something strange. I'm at the back of the retail strip, where the shop's back door opens to an alleyway and a dumpster. The door's ajar but there are no lights on. Like someone forgot to lock or close it properly.

I head over, frowning. Is Adele inside? And she just forgot to shut the door behind her? Doesn't seem like something my conscientious and responsible friend would do. But her loosey-goosey business partner is another story.

"Hello?" I call, pushing the door open. I wait a beat but there's no answer. I frown and pull the door shut, making sure it's secure. It's not locked but that's the best I can do. I shoot off a text to Adele real quick.

Hey, are you at the shop? The back door was open. But no lights are on.

I kick around in the back alley for a minute or so to see if Adele will text back. A cold wind snakes up as I wait. The temperature's dropped with the sun so I turn up my collar. I should have put on more layers or a scarf before leaving the house. Will the baby be okay in the cold? It's still so little in my belly. There are so many things I don't know about being a mom.

I check my phone and there's still no text from Adele so I keep walking. Hopefully she'll see the text and come by to lock the shop properly. Weird that it was left unlocked—probably Bing being an idiot.

I'm a few steps down the alley when I sense someone behind me. I half turn but there are only shadows.

"Hello?" I call, but there's no movement around the dumpsters. I could have sworn some was there. I rub the back of my neck. I got the same sort of feeling when the wolf was following me. Of course that wolf was really Lance, and look how that turned out.

I'm halfway down the alley when there's a roar of an engine and a large van turns into the alleyway. Its lights are off.

"Hey," I shout, to make sure the driver knows I'm here, even as I scuttle to the side of the alley, heading to safety near a cluster of dumpsters. I'm facing the dark van, walking backwards, when I bump into something warm and solid.

"Oh!" I whirl and recoil. A shadowy shape looms closer —a man in a ski mask. *What the—?* I startle away, nearly falling. My cell phone falls out of my hand and spins across the pavement. I would dive for it, but the thug's still coming at me.

I turn to run, but the van blocks my escape. Its lights are still off, and in the darkness, trapped between the thug and the van, I slowly realize what's happening. I open my mouth to scream when the thug lunges and strikes me in the head, and the world goes dark.

~

Lance

I give up knocking on the front door and head to the back, adrenaline pumping. Charlie hasn't answered texts or calls. I shoot a text to Deke: *Has Sadie heard from Charlie? She's not answering her calls.*

I know she wanted space, but when she didn't text me back, I got worried. I wrack my brain, trying to figure out where else she might have gone.

Deke replies: *Sadie hasn't. Channing's on it.* Channing can track her cell.

I force open the back door and walk briskly through the house. Lights off, place quiet. No sign of Charlie. My wolf is restless.

"Take it easy," I say aloud. "She's fine. She's just taking a walk. Or running an errand—without her car."

My phone rings. When I answer, Channing says, without waiting for a greeting, "Cell data says she's in Taos. Pinpointing now."

I trot out of the house and down the sidewalk, forcing myself not to break into a run. *She's fine. She's fine.*

"She's near The Chocolatier. Adele's shop."

Relief. I break into a jog anyway, my wolf desperate to see Charlie. When I'm by the shop, I redial Channing. "Where?"

He doesn't need clarification. "Around the back. In the alley. I'll ring it."

I race around the back. Charlie's scent is back here, a mix of old and new, but no Charlie. The bottom of my stomach drops, and dread crawls over my skin.

Fuck. There's no phone ringing. I pace down the alleyway, catching Charlie's sweet scent. I don't have to shift into the wolf to use my nose. Scents are clearer when I'm in wolf form, but I won't risk someone spotting a giant wolf near the plaza. Not unless I have to.

Then I spot it—over by a cluster of dumpsters. The phone is cracked, but it's Charlie's. It smells like her. There's another scent nearby—someone with a greasy, diesel-fume scent.

A growl bursts out of me. I can't hold it back. My wolf is fucking frantic. I clutch the phone and crouch to the pavement where there are traces of her scent, and the faint lingering scents of two strange men. The trail ends in the alleyway where the diesel scent is strongest.

Something's wrong. Charlie's gone.

∼

Charlie

SLOWLY, I come to. There's clear air washing over my face, alternating with blasts of diesel fumes. There's a gag stretching my mouth and I'm tied tight with my hands behind me, lying on my side. Sharp pain radiates through my head from a spot in my skull. When I try to open my eyes, I retch a little into the dank wad of cloth filling my mouth.

Oh God, the baby. I hunch as if I can protect my abdomen. My insides feel fine—as fine as they can feel with me tied up and desperate for water. The ropes tying me bite into my skin and my sides throb with a collection of bruises I didn't have before I woke, but I'm alive. For now.

What happened? My head throbs as I review… the shop, the strange men, a blow to the head. Did I interrupt a robbery? What is going on?

I wonder for what feels like hours. Eventually, the truck rumbles to a stop. In the sudden quiet, I try to scream, but my throat is too dry and the gag muffles all sound.

A sharp sound of a canvas flap being drawn aside, and a bright light calls across my face.

A man swears. "You fucked up taking her. Black Wolf's going to be on our ass."

"Who?"

The light cuts off and the canvas falls, swallowing the rest of the conversation. I strain but all I hear are murmurs. I flex my fingers, trying to test my bonds, but they hold tight, chafing my skin.

Black Wolf's going to be on our ass. Does this have something to do with Black Wolf Security? Hope blazes in my chest like a flare in the dark. Lance and his pack will save me. They have to. The alternative is unthinkable.

But as the truck rumbles on and I shiver with the cold and sick adrenaline, another thought settles in. What if I was kidnapped *because* of Black Wolf?

Lance and his pack are into very dangerous business. I saw the way his body was riddled with bullet holes. If someone found out he had a mate, or worse, a child, our family would be a target. For leverage. For revenge. For any number of things I don't even want to think about.

Lance

I tear into pack HQ, chest heaving like I ran from town instead of racing like a maniac and leaving my Ducati lying on its side on our front lawn.

"Update?" I bark, bursting into the operations room.

Channing's big form is hunched in front of a display of screens. He's got huge headphones on and doesn't notice my arrival. Rafe intercepts me, a hollow look to his face.

"We've got visual from security cam footage." Rafe leads me into his office. "Security cameras in the alley picked this up." He points a remote at a screen mounted on the wall. The blurry footage is a small square in the center, but it clearly shows Charlie's limp body being loaded into a nondescript van by two hooded men.

I throw back my head and howl. My wolf crawls under my skin, threatening to burst out. But that won't help Charlie. I need to stay in human form.

"Steady," Rafe orders, stepping close.

I grit my teeth, every muscle flexing. I want to wreck myself, scream, run a thousand miles. Anything to save Charlie and my pup. Anything to stop the constant litany pounding through my head. *My fault. My fault she was taken. My fault they're in danger.*

"It's not your fault, soldier," Rafe barks, and I realize I said my litany out loud.

"They took her, I know they took her." I'm pacing. "We need to find out where."

"We don't know who they are."

"It's gotta be Vincent Sarcero." I name the arms dealer we robbed in our last job. "He figured it out, he's hunting us down for revenge. Fuck!" I explode and punch the wall. The drywall dents under my hand in an explosion of white dust.

"Get it together, soldier," Rafe orders, and I turn on him with a snarl. He growls back louder, and it steadies my wolf somewhat. My brother's dominant alpha presence helps. "We don't know shit right now. And going full wolf won't help Charlie."

He's right. Fuck. I've got to hold it together.

"What do we know about ground zero?" Rafe asks. He means the site of the kidnapping.

I straighten and report, "There were scents of two men. The ones from the video. No one else. All the other scents were older." I scrub a hand over my face. "They could be far out of town by now."

"I've called in every favor. Channing was able to pull plates from the van, and police are on alert. Channing's monitoring their scanner."

"What else?"

"I have calls in to the Colonel and the Kings…" His voice dies as Deke steps into the doorway, his arms around Sadie. The petite human woman sees the spot where I punched the wall and her eyes widen.

"Tell us what you know, baby," Deke murmurs.

Sadie swallows twice and drags her eyes away from the wall. "I called Adele, and it went to voicemail. Tabitha is heading over to her house now."

"The shop was unlocked," I said. "They could've lured her in, been waiting for her." I run a hand through my hair, shaking with the urge to shift.

Rafe puts a hand on my shoulder. "Conserve your energy. We'll have a target soon."

"I've got intel," Channing calls. "Kylie King's online."

We crowd into the operations room, where one of the screens shows Kylie King's pale face. She doesn't look like the relaxed mom Charlie and I saw onscreen in Cabo. Her hair's pulled back and her face is scrunched, her eyes shaded by yellow rimless glasses. There's a furious clatter of keys as she types.

"I'm trolling the darknet right now," she reports without looking up. "I've got searches flagging any mention of Charlie, Black Wolf Security, and anything in the vicinity of Taos."

"What about Vincent Sarcero?" I cut in.

Kylie wrinkles her nose and shakes her head. "There's a rumor that he's dead."

"Dead?" Deke and I echo at the same time.

"Nothing confirmed. Not yet," Kylie says. "I'm working on it. Give me a bit. I'll get you more."

"Thanks, Kylie," Rafe says.

"Of course." Kylie spares a second to look at the screen. Her face goes soft for a moment when she sees me. "We'll get her back, Lance."

I manage a nod before Kylie's screen goes dark.

Rafe steps in front of the screens, holding up his phone. "Just got off the line with Colonel Johnson. A strike team was successful in taking out Vincent Sarcero early this morning. His organization is in chaos."

"No shit," Deke rumbles. "So it can't be him."

"Not unless he gave the order before his death. But I doubt it."

Vincent Sarcero was at the top of my list of suspects. If he didn't have Charlie kidnapped, who did?

Charlie

After a long drive that lasts forever, the truck slows and stops. A few dogs bark, and a man shouts at them until they shut up.

Fuck. I listen for clues of where I am and who's taken me, but I'm freaking out.

The bed ramp lowers with a clang. Rough hands drag me out. I writhe, but I can't really move or fight.

"Easy, sweetheart," one of the guys mutters, lifting me against him. I pant against the gag, my head growing light as a balloon. I dig my nails into my palms, trying to slow my breath.

While I'm trying to keep from hyperventilating, the guy

carries me into a dark warehouse. He weaves around some vehicles and equipment.

"This her?" another guy asks. My captor grunts.

Chills run up and down my spine. *Her?* They were looking for *me?* The idea that this is somehow related to Lance's business takes hold again. But if it is, he'll find me. He won't let us—me and his pup—die. Or at least he will do everything in his power to get us back. I feel certain of that.

I just have to survive. *Please, please, Lance. Come quick.*

"In here." The second man kicks open a door and the first carries me inside, setting me on the concrete floor. There are some pieces of trash but nothing else—nothing but darkness and the sharp, sour scent of my own sweat.

The door shuts and I'm left, still tied and gagged, to ponder my fate.

Lance

I stare at the screens in the operations room, wishing I could help. My wolf has settled. The sick feeling in my stomach is gone, replaced by the cool numbness I feel right before battle. It's quiet now, the only sound coming from Channing's thick fingers dancing over the keyboard. For a big fucker who resembles a bulldozer more than a nerd, he's pretty good on computers.

I jump as Kylie flickers back on screen. "I'm getting some movement in Taos. Does anybody know a Christopher Ford?" she asks.

"Yeah," Rafe says. "That's Adele's business partner. He's fifty percent owner of her chocolate shop."

"You mean Bing?" Sadie asks.

"Right," Rafe confirms. "He's a pothead and a small-time

dealer, but he's harmless. I ran a thorough check on him a while back." Of course he did. Rafe wouldn't be my big brother if he wasn't a super paranoid control freak. Although why he was trying to control Adele's life is unclear. It doesn't matter— right now, I love him for it.

"Well, it looks like he graduated from pot to meth, at least in the past few months," Kylie reports. "He's gotten involved with some bad guys. Like, really bad guys. There's a bounty on his head."

Sadie gasps and Deke pulls her back against him, steadying her with an arm around her waist.

"I'll alert the cops," Rafe rasps, stepping out of the room with his cell to his ear.

Fuck, is it possible this wasn't anything to do with our mission? That some punk got mixed up in some shit and Charlie was just in the wrong place at the wrong time?

Minutes crawl past.

"Fuck," Channing says, pulling his headphones down. "Police scanner's on fire. They're outside Christopher Ford's place. There's a body."

I surge to my feet with a roar.

Charlie

The longer I lie on the concrete floor, the colder I get. Not much I can do about it. *Please, please, little baby. Please be okay. Mommy's gonna figure this out.*

I squeeze my eyes shut. I can't cry. I need the moisture. I remember what Lance said. Shifter babies are strong, right? I can be strong for my baby.

But I jerk when the door creaks open and a little light pours in. My heart strangles itself in my chest.

"She's awake," the guy says to someone. He crouches next to me. He's left the ski mask off this time. He's a white guy with a dirty beard and bland features. He reaches for me and I flinch. Not like I can get up and run away. But he cuffs one wrist to a ring set in the cement floor and then slices off the ropes. I scuttle back as fast as I can—not very fast—and lean against the wall. I claw the gag out myself. I wish I could spit out the awful taste but my mouth's too dry.

"Here." He holds out a bottle of water. He waits until I'm watching and twists off the top. But when he holds it out, I don't move. With a small sigh, he sets it down on the floor and scoots back so I can grab it for myself. I force myself to move slowly, holding the bottle with both hands. The first taste is heaven and I let it wet my mouth before drinking deeply.

"That's better," he murmurs. "We got off on the wrong foot."

No shit, Sherlock. I squint at him and he shrugs. "Things didn't go down how we wanted. It's nothing personal. But you've got something that we want."

"What?" My voice is still scratchy.

"The account numbers. Your business partner owes us a lot of money."

My business partner? My head throbs as I try to think. What business? I'm a postal worker.

My captor is still talking. "He was supposed to meet us and give us what he owed. But he didn't show, and you did."

Then I remember: The Chocolatier's door had been open. These guys grabbed me just outside of it. Do they think I'm Adele?

"You mean Bing?" I rasp.

He cocks his head. "Yeah, him."

"But I don't know him," I say.

The man's face hardens, and I press my back to the wall.

"Listen, sweetheart, if you cooperate, it's going to go a lot easier for you. We already took out your partner."

What? "Bing is dead?"

"That's what happens when you fuck with us. But if you cooperate with us, we'll let you go."

I stare at him, panting through my open mouth, trying to hold my shit together. This guy is lying. I've seen his face. If I hand over the information he wants, I'm fucked.

But I'm fucked either way. What are they going to do when they find out I'm not Adele?

~

Lance

The street outside Christopher Ford's condo is full of cop cars. We're in the Humvee and we can't even get close. I sit frozen in the front seat, the blue and red lights washing over my face, waiting for Rafe to return. My brother decided to drive to the crime scene, and he wanted me close by. Better than sitting and twiddling my thumbs, waiting for intel. Channing will call as soon as we know what's going down.

Rafe jogs back, weaving between cop cars to hop in the Humvee's driver's seat. "I couldn't get near the body. But it's definitely a hit."

I growl and grab the door handle. Let the cops try and stop a three hundred pound wolf from getting close.

"Don't," Rafe orders. "It won't do any good to get closer. Cops will just arrest you. Now that we know Charlie was taken in relation to this, Channing and Kylie can track these fuckers. As soon as we have intel, we move out." His phone buzzes and he has it to his ear in less than a second. "Lightfoot."

"Sadie got a call," Deke growls into the phone.

"Tabitha just left me a message," Sadie says. "She needs help. The police just picked up Adele for questioning about the murder of her business partner."

"Fuck," Rafe shouts, sending a blast of alpha energy through all of us.

So he does have an interest in Adele. Or some kind of stake in this. He slams the car into gear.

~

Charlie

A calm settles over me.

"I'm not Adele," I say. "And I can prove it to you." I raise my hand slowly and point to my jacket pocket. "I'm going to pull out my wallet."

He nods and I pull it out, tossing it to the floor by his feet.

"I'm Charlie Archman. I work for the US Postal system," I say quickly.

"Fuck," the man says. His grubby fingers claw at my ID. He rises and slams the door behind him. I sag back in the dark.

Kidnapping a postal worker is pretty bad. But if the guy tries to mess with me, I'll tell him I'm dating Lance Lightfoot of Black Wolf Security, and he'll realize how well and truly fucked he is.

This situation wasn't Lance's fault. I'm not sure if that's a relief or more worrisome, because I don't even know if Lance knows I'm missing. I'd told him I wanted some space tonight. He might be giving it to me. Hell, it could be until tomorrow when I don't show up for work before anyone knows I'm missing.

Lance

When we arrive back at HQ, Deke is piling gear on the lawn. He's in tactical gear, with black greasepaint smeared over his face. Sadie stands a few feet away, arms wrapped around herself. As soon as we park, Rafe jumps out and opens the door for Adele. She steps out, head held high, followed by Tabitha. Sadie sees them and races over for a group hug.

"Inside," Rafe barks. I help him herd the ladies into HQ. Rafe called in more favors and got Adele released while I nearly clawed the inside of the vehicle apart.

Channing rises to greet us, pulling off his headphones.

"What's going on?" I ask. "Have you found her?"

"Got a lead on where they might be holding her. Carson National Forest. Teddy's on his way," Channing reports.

Thank fuck.

"Gear up," Rafe orders, and Channing and I race from the room. This is the moment I've been waiting for. *I'm coming, Charlie. Hang on.*

The human women are gathered on the porch when I trot out. Far in the distance, I hear the sounds of a chopper coming closer.

"This is my fault," Adele is saying. "This has something to do with Bing." Her friends are on either side of her, hugging her.

But Rafe stops in front of her. "There's nothing you could have done. Don't take responsibility for what the enemy does. This is all on their heads."

Adele nods but doesn't look convinced. "So what's the plan?"

"We've got an idea of where she's being held. We're going

to go, and we're going to bring her back." And Rafe does something I've never thought I'd see him do. He catches Adele's chin and raises her face to meet his gaze. "I promise you, we're going to bring her back."

Teddy's got the bird hovering right overhead now, the wind from the clacking blades shaking the trees around our lawn.

"But how—" Adele shouts and Rafe puts a finger to her lips.

"We're going to do what we do. Stay here. Stay safe." He backs away, waving to us. "Move out!"

Charlie

A SMALL NOISE WAKES ME, and I twitch. My muscles are sore and stiff from sitting. Not that I can do much with my wrist handcuffed to the floor. At least I'm not still tied up.

There's no light sneaking under the door. Is it morning yet? After I finished my water, I curled up best I could and shut my eyes. I must be seriously dehydrated because I haven't had to pee. Not sure if that's a good or a bad thing.

I sense rather than hear a presence outside the door. There's a whisper of sound, and I stiffen. Is the guy returning?

The door creaks open and a large shadow slips inside. Glittering eyes in a paint-mottled face loom in front of me, and a gentle hand settles over my mouth, stifling my cry.

"Charlie." His arms are strong around me. My breath rattles in my throat as I press my face against his chest, breathing him in. Is this a dream?

"Angel, I'm here," Lance's voice is a bare whisper. "We're going to get you out now. It's gonna be okay." He pats me down lightly, sniffing along my neck. "Are you hurt?"

"No," I croak. I try to put my arms around him, and the handcuffs clank. A growl rumbles deep in his chest under my ear.

"Hang on." There's a sound like a crumpling tin can and then my arm can move freely. The cuff is still around my wrist but the chain is gone.

Lance scoops me into his arms like a groom carrying a bride. "Hang on to me, angel. We're sneaking out."

The door moves slightly and two glowing green eyes flash up at us. I startle and Lance breathes in my ear, "Easy. It's just Rafe."

I can just make out the giant black wolf just outside the door. It dips its head and slinks away.

"He'll go first," Lance whispers.

I nod and press my face against his neck, sucking in lung-fuls of his scent to keep me grounded. Lance has camo paint mottling his face and coating his light hair. He's a demon in the night. But not as scary as that big black wolf.

"You ready?"

I squeeze him tighter, not trusting myself to speak. His muscles flex under me and then we're on the run. The wind on my face tells me we're moving faster than any human could run. In a few moments, we're outside the warehouse. A dog barks in the distance, but otherwise the night is still.

A ten foot tall fence topped with razor wire surrounds the compound, the metal glittering silver in the moonlight. Ahead of us, a black wolf leaps over it in a graceful, impossible ballet that takes my breath away.

"Catch her," Lance mutters. The wolf suddenly shifts and

takes human form. Rafe is clothed in some kind of stretchy material that serves as boxers, so he's not naked.

"Ready, Charlie?"

"Um…"

Lance swings me into the air like he's tossing a sack of potatoes. I squeeze my eyes shut and brace for the catch. Rafe catches me so easily, there's barely an impact, and then Lance vaults over the fence, easily clearing the razor wire. I gape, transfixed by his prowess. Is this what it's like, being a shifter? Will our baby be like this?

Behind us, the dogs have started to make a racket. Rafe shifts back to wolf form.

"Shit." Lance scoops me up and weaves through the forest. I peek for a second, growing dizzy at the sight of trees blurring past us. "We're not out of the woods yet," he says.

"What's going to happen?"

"I wanted to light that place up," he tells me. "Turn it into scorched earth. But Rafe vetoed a strike. In a few hours, that place will be crawling with cops."

"I meant how do we get out of here?"

"Oh. That's the fun part." His grin is as big as ever. I'm the most scared I've been in my life and Lance is smiling. This is another day on the job for him. He lives in this world —his entire adult life has been spent in danger.

Fun part?

Lance stops and crouches behind a boulder, with me still in his arms.

Someone crouches next to us. "There she is." White flashes between the dark camo paint—Channing giving me a grin. He hands me a bottle of water. Lance helps me hold it as I suck the liquid down as slowly as I can.

"Easy, angel." Lance pats my back when I gasp and sputter. "I've got you."

I hug him tight, squeezing my eyes to keep the tears in. I'm safe now. Lance got me out. It's going to be okay.

"All right, get ready to run," Channing mutters. He stashes the empty bottle in a pack and pulls out a walkie-talkie. "Echo-1, this is Alpha-10 requesting pickup."

Lance shifts me in his arms so Channing can hand him the device. "Echo 1, we've got the package. Time to FedEx the hell out," Lance repeats. Behind us, back at the compound, lights have flooded on. The sounds of dogs are getting louder.

"Roger that." The walkie-talkie buzzes with the static-filled reply. "Echo-1 on its way. Alpha-10 stand by."

When I look back down, there's a big wolf with white patches where Channing was standing. The wolf gives me a grin, picks up the pack in his mouth, and bounds away.

"This is it, baby. Almost outta here." Lance rises and sets off. We're on a mountain, and he's taking us to higher ground. There's the dull thunder of chopper blades up ahead. A helicopter hovers over a rocky outcropping. And we're rushing straight toward it.

"Hang on." Lance kicks into real speed, and trees fly by. We crash through the brush and up towards the waiting helicopter. Teddy's come through. But there's no sign of the black, or brown and white wolf. No Rafe, no Channing.

"What about the others?" I cry over the roar of the engine and wind from the rotors.

"They can take care of themselves," Lance shouts. He leaps into the chopper and settles into a seat, holding me tight. He straps his own body to the seat one arm at a time, still holding me. I don't think he'll ever let me go.

"I'm so sorry, angel," he says. I don't know how I hear him over the roar of the blades, but I do. "It's almost over."

My teeth are chattering with cold and adrenaline, but I'm alive. We're airborne, flying away into the night.

But before I can sigh in relief, there's a long, low whistling sound that grows into a horrible whine. Then impact. The chopper shudders and lurches to the side.

"Fuck." Lance grips me tighter.

"Abort mission," Teddy yells. Everything moves in slow motion. I can barely see in the shadows, but I feel Lance reach behind us and grab something. Before I know it, we're out of the seat and Lance is strapping me to him.

"What are you doing?" I scream.

"We're going down," Lance shouts.

No. We can't be going down. I'm not ready to die. Not when I have so much to live for—this tiny life growing inside me means everything to me.

The helicopter tips, and we lurch against the seat. I scream, and my stomach swoops. The helicopter plummets toward the ground.

"Hang on!" Lance's grip on me is brutal. Wind slaps my face; I can barely see. Lance heaves us to the open side of the chopper and leaps out. My screams are lost in the rush of air.

I can't die. Please don't let me die. Please, God, let me and this baby live. I'll do anything to protect it.

The world is suddenly silent. We float in the night, the stars twinkling above. It's almost peaceful in this rush of wind. And then somehow Lance turns us and I'm facing down over the valley. We are fucking falling. Free falling. We're gonna fucking die.

I scream his name as another whine pierces the quiet.

Far above us, the helicopter explodes. A sharp blast, a piercing boom. Light splintering the night. Lance hunches over me. I'm strapped to him somehow but I clutch him tight.

"Hold on to me, Charlie." The words drift slowly through the ringing in my ears. My face is numb. The night wind is cold, sharp as a blade, and then a huge jerk makes my heart stop. The parachute unfurls above us. We hang in the air, high above the valley. Below us, the roads and houses are twinkling lights mirroring the stars.

"I've got you, angel." Lance's eyes are a beacon in the night. "I've got you." He holds me tight as we float to earth.

～

Charlie

Day dawns bright and cold. Lance and I ride in the back of a big black Yukon. After we landed, Lance got us free of the parachute, picked me up, and walked us to the road. It wasn't long before Deke drove up with Teddy already in the front seat.

"Rafe and Channing got out safe," Deke reported immediately. "The cops have already stormed the compound. Found a fucking grenade launcher."

"Yeah, we figured that out." Teddy chuckles. For a guy who got his chopper shot out from under him, he's pretty chill. His huge body is stuffed into the passenger side and every time he moves, the seat creaks, but he's relaxed and grinning like he's on vacation.

Me? I can't stop shaking. I'm in Lance's arms, tucked against his side. My teeth keep chattering, too.

"Are you cold, angel?" Lance asks.

I shrug. My skin is numb. Lance meets Deke's eyes in the rearview mirror. Deke nods and punches a bunch of buttons. A second later, hot air comes blasting out and Lance points the blowers at me.

But I can't feel anything.

"We'll go to the hospital. Get you checked out. And the baby."

"Right." My voice sounds far away. My ears keep

popping—probably from the blast. The blast from a freaking helicopter exploding right above me.

"I'm so sorry, angel," he says, even though none of this was his fault. Even though he's the one who saved me. He kisses my temple for the millionth time.

I want to let him take care of me, the way he just did. The way he has since the moment we met. But I can't seem to let him in. It's like the fear seeped into my bones, and won't leave.

CHAPTER 15

THE NEXT MORNING, Charlie stirs against my chest. She was a million miles away yesterday as we dealt with the aftermath of her abduction. Withdrawn. Seemingly numb. Almost blank.

It's scared the hell out of me—and nothing scares me.

To make it worse, she had nightmares during the night, waking up with startled cries, trembling in my arms as I held her and reminded her she was safe.

Now, she blinks her eyes open and then her gaze slides away from me. My pulse picks up speed.

"Charlie? Talk to me, angel. I know you're not okay."

She sits up and swings her legs over the side of the bed, giving me her back. She's in one of her threadbare graphic tees and a pair of panties. There was no love-making last night and it seems like there won't be any this morning, either.

She sighs. "No, I'm not." When she turns to look at me, there's pain in her eyes. "Lance, what happened to me was sort of a wake-up call. I…" She runs a hand over her face. "I can't deal with high-stress situations. Not when I have the baby to think about."

"Of course you're not, angel. No one should have to deal with what happened to you. It was fucked up."

Her lips turn inside, pressed together, and she slumps her shoulders. "*You* can deal with it." I don't know why her words sound like an accusation rather than an accolade.

"I'm nearly indestructible, Charlie, and I trained in the military my entire adult life. I've been in situations like that before."

"Yeah," she mumbles. "I sort of got the feeling you're in situations like that on a monthly basis."

I stare at her, concrete filling my trunk. Where is she going with this?

"Am I right?" she demands.

I nod. "Yeah. But like I said, I'm not human. It's different."

Charlie turns her head away, blinking rapidly. My body tightens. My mate is crying—because of me. "I don't want to think about you out there crashing to your death in flaming helicopters. Or getting every part of your body shot up. I mean, you said *nearly* indestructible. You can be killed, can't you?"

I throw my hands in the air, getting up from the bed. "Charlie, anyone can be killed at any time. You can't dwell on it."

Charlie gets up, too, tugging on her own fingers. "It's not what I want," she blurts.

I go still. "What do you mean?" I ask softly, dread creeping through my veins with icy tentacles.

"I had a plan, remember?" Her eyes are still brimming with unshed tears, and her voice trembles.

I try to swallow, and fail. "I remember."

"My life was supposed to be boring and stable. I want that life back. I need it." She's twisting her fingers together now and it breaks my heart. I want to go to her and fold her into my arms, but she's still backing away. "I can't take the worry. I grew up always worrying whether one parent or the other would make it back. And now Chad, too. I can't do that with you. And I don't want our child to have to live that life, either."

"Charlie…" I start to walk around the bed, but she holds up her hand.

"Please. Just let me get this out." Now the tears spill, two down one cheek, another down the side of her nose. "Lance, when I got kidnapped yesterday, the kidnappers mentioned Black Wolf."

I frown.

"I think it's just because they were scared of you guys, but at the time, I thought maybe I was being kidnapped *because* of you. Because someone found out I was your mate and they wanted to use me to get to you."

I scrub a hand across my face. "Yeah, I thought that, too," I admit.

Biggest mistake ever. Charlie's eyes widen and she covers her mouth, stumbling back. "I was right," she chokes out.

"No, wait—right about what?" I move into her space, but still don't touch her. She's too closed off—her arm wrapped around her waist protectively.

"What you do… your missions… they're dangerous. And that puts me in danger. That puts our baby in danger."

191

"No—" I say, but it's a lie. She's right. She's absolutely right, and it's like a knife to the gut.

"Lance, I can't do this. You're amazing in bed. You're incredibly sweet and protective, but it's not enough," she whispers. "This wasn't what I wanted. It's not what I need."

My heart tumbles out of my chest and thunks to the floor at our feet.

"I'll be whatever you need, Charlie," I say across the dry ashes in my mouth.

"You can't. I'm sorry, Lance. I'm…" She gestures at nothing. "Sunsets in Cabo are nice, but they're not enough."

I'm not enough. Rafe was right. I don't have what it takes to be a dad.

Getting shot was less painful than this.

My wolf is howling so loud, I barely hear Charlie's next words. "I'm going to go."

Panic squeezes my chest. "What? Where?"

"I have a plan. I can stay with my parents in Arizona. They're retired now. They can help me take care of the baby when it's born." She's already turning away, pushing the closet doors open and pulling out two suitcases.

Alarm bells clang through my head, drowning out my wolf. Heat floods my body, nearly making me shift—not from anger, but out of the perceived danger. I'm losing my mate. I'm losing my mate and my pup.

And I can't stop it.

"When?" I manage to say as I watch her throw clothes into the suitcase.

"Um, right away. I just think a clean break will be easier for both of us. After what happened, I need to get some distance between me and Taos. I thought this would be a good place to raise kids, but I was totally wrong."

I don't tell her that leaving me is an impossibility. I mean, she can leave, but I will follow.

But that would only upset her. I need to give her space. She just said she needs a clean break. Distance. I'll have to hold my wolf back from trailing right after her.

I don't know how I'll do it—the instinct to protect her and that unborn pup is so strong, it might kill me. Can a mated wolf go moon mad?

Fuck.

"Okay," I hear myself say over the rushing in my ears. "I understand." I pull on my clothes. It's a lie. I don't understand. I don't understand anything.

Or maybe I do.

Rafe was right all along. If I'm not responsible enough to take care of myself, how could I imagine I'm responsible enough to take care of a mate and pup? Charlie doesn't think I can handle it, that's obvious.

I'm the guy she had fun with. The guy she calls for good sex and lots of orgasms, but I'm not the guy she wants to settle down with. I'm not the guy she trusts to keep her and her family safe. I'm not the doctor or dentist or CPA who knows how to coach Little League and has never held a gun.

I stick my feet in my boots. "Can I help you pack?" My voice sounds raspy and tired.

Charlie shakes her head. "No." There are tears in her voice. "It would be easier for me if you left."

I step in with the urge to kiss her head or temple before I go, but she stiffens and I stop.

Fuck.

"Goodbye," I murmur as I walk to the door.

"Bye," she chokes out.

And then it's over.

~

Charlie

I THROW up as soon as Lance leaves. After I've retched, I start bawling. I had no idea breaking up could feel so awful. But I can't do this.

I call Sadie to come over and help me pack. Tabitha's staying with Adele—and after what Adele's been through, I don't want to bug her. Her business partner's dead, and she was questioned about his murder. She's going through enough.

But when my doorbell rings, all three of my friends are standing outside. And I fall apart all over again.

We spend all morning and half the afternoon getting everything important for the short term shoved into my Subaru. The rest I can come back and get when I sell the house. Or when my heart isn't breaking into a million shattered pieces and I am able to think straight.

"Are you sure this is the right thing?" Sadie keeps asking. "I mean, look at you." She gestures at me with her forehead wrinkled in concern. "You haven't stopped crying all day."

"I know. It's the hormones. I'm sure."

"I don't think it's just the hormones." Adele cocks a hip, but her face is also creased with worry. "Charlie, you had a big scare. You could've died, and it was my fault." Adele blinks, her jaw taut.

"No it wasn't," I interrupt.

"I never should've gotten involved with Bing. That was supposed to be me they kidnapped."

"That doesn't make it your fault!" I exclaim. "This isn't about fault. It was just a wake-up call to me about what kind of life I want to provide for my child. I *need* stability. I need to be with my parents in their quiet little retirement community, where nothing exciting happens and everyone wants to make a baby smile."

"I don't think children are even allowed to live in retirement communities," Tabitha says slowly.

I pause. She might be right. "Well, my parents will help me figure it out. Can you watch Merlin for me for a little while?"

"Of course," Tabitha says.

"Thanks." I force a smile. "I'll get him when I move."

"But what about your job? What about… us?" Sadie asks in a small voice. Adele puts an arm around her and Sadie moves closer, sniffling. Fuck, we're all going to be crying by the time I drive out of here.

I cross the room and put my hands on Sadie's shoulders. "I love you guys. I do. I love you so much. But I really need to go. I need… time." And space.

"What about Lance?" Tabitha asks.

Pain in my chest, like I've been knifed. I grit my teeth against it before answering. "I don't want to talk about him."

"Charlie…" Adele stops. "Drive safely. Call me when you get there if you want to talk."

"Me too," Sadie says.

"Me three." Tabitha folds me into her arms.

I try to swallow the fresh wave of sobs hitting me. I give each of them a hug. "Thank you all. Thank you so much. I'll be in touch."

I climb in the Subaru, and start the engine.

As I pull out, I catch sight of a pair of silver-blue eyes glinting from behind the bushes at my fence.

Lance.

I gulp down a sob. Again.

And then I drive away.

～

Lance

After Charlie drives away, I have Teddy fly me a hundred miles into the wilderness and drop me off. I figure it's the only way I can keep from following her, and mere survival will keep my wolf busy for a while.

Four days later, I limp onto Black Wolf property, my paws bloody and raw, my fur matted with snow.

Rafe storms out of our place when he sees me. "Shift," he commands.

My human form feels even worse than my wolf form. Ragged and worn. Barely hanging on.

Rafe punches me in the nose, and I go down on my bare ass in the snow. "You selfish fucking bastard," he snarls.

Blood spurts from my broken nose.

"I didn't fucking know if you were going to live or die out there."

I drag myself to my feet and snort, sending droplets of blood flying. "Right. Because Fate knows I'm not capable of surviving on my own."

Rafe's mouth turns down and his shoulders sag. "Fuck, Lance." He pulls me into a rough hug.

I don't hug him back.

I'm capable of anything but standing on my feet and filling my lungs with air.

"She'll come around," he tells me.

I pull away and give my head a shake. "Will she? I really don't know."

And then suddenly, as I'm standing there, it all becomes clear. What I need to do to get my mate back.

Leave Rafe. Leave my pack. Leave this life that she objects to.

I can't have both—Charlie made that clear. She doesn't want to raise a child with a mercenary for a father. She wants plain and boring and safe.

She doesn't think I can be that, but I can. I will.

"I'm out," I say.

"What?" Rafe's brows lower. Deke and Channing come out to stand behind him on the wooden porch.

"Charlie isn't down with this." I circle my finger at our property. "And I need to take care of my family. I have my own pack now."

Rafe's expression flickers between confusion and grief. "Fuck."

"Fuck," Channing echoes.

"Lance," Deke says, but doesn't follow up with anything.

I walk up the steps, pushing past them. "I've gotta go. I'm not your responsibility anymore. I'm not letting Charlie have that baby on her own."

"You're right." Rafe's voice behind me makes me stop. I turn. "Of course you're right. Fuck."

"I'm sorry." I shake my head. "I don't want to let you guys down, but they have to come first."

"They do," Deke says in a deep rumble.

"Definitely," Channing agrees.

I walk to my room to get in the shower. I need to clean up, eat some food, and pack.

I'm moving to Arizona.

harlie

"CHARLIE, hon, I think I should take you to the doctor. All this puking can't be good for the baby," my mom says, her hand on my upper back as I bend over the toilet and dry heave.

If Lance were here he would've made sure I'd eaten enough before I got to this point.

That thought sends me into a spiral of fresh grief.

I thought that being with my family would somehow make everything magically better. Or at least make sense. I guess I associated having children with my own family, but now that I'm here with my parents in Green Valley, I feel lonelier than ever. Or maybe it's the ache in my heart that won't go away.

I applied for a job with the postal service here and in Tucson, but there aren't any openings at the moment. I've spent the last week helping my mom with her gardening, crying, and throwing up.

So yeah, it's been fun. Heartbroken, pregnant, living with my parents again. Oh, and puking a lot. One star, do not recommend.

"I'm okay. I just need to force some food down. Are there any more crackers?"

"I'll check and see, hon."

I sigh and wash my face in the sink.

When I come out, my mom has poured a sleeve of crackers into a Tupperware bowl, which she sets on the table. I plunk down on a chair and pick one up. She sits across from me.

"Have you talked to him?"

I shake my head. "No."

Frankly, I'm surprised he hasn't contacted me. But then, I saw the hurt on his face when I broke up with him. What had I said? I can't even remember—I was so raw with emotion and hormones.

Just thinking of him makes me cry again. I miss having him close. His easy-going grin. The safety I feel in his strong arms. The way he makes me smile, relaxes me, takes care of me.

The cracker is dry on my tongue. "I think I made a mistake, Mom."

"With Lance?"

I nod. "With leaving. I thought being near you and Dad would be the best place to raise a child, but now…"

"A child needs their father," my mom says.

I slump in my chair. "I didn't have a father half the time. And half the time, I didn't have a mother," I say. "It was terrifying growing up worrying one of you might never come back."

"Oh, Charlie." My mom's eyes glitter with tears. "I'm sorry you suffered. We suffered too. You think it didn't kill us every time to ship out and leave the most precious thing known to us behind? I mean, I knew your father would take good care of you, but would he do the things I would for you? And then I had to miss all those months of you growing up. Time I'll never ever get back."

"I know. I just don't want my child to worry about his or her father like that. And Lance is in a dangerous business. He and his brother are mercenaries—they could get killed any time."

But I remember that's not really true. Lance told me he's nearly indestructible. And I saw how quickly he healed from dozens of gunshot wounds.

"There is no perfect, Charlie. Your dad and I did the best we could. That's all you and Lance can do, too."

I let her words wash over me, realizing how true they are. My mom was younger than I was when she got pregnant with me. She was in the Air Force, which made starting a family less than ideal. She wanted better for us, but she did what she could.

"I get that you want to shield your child from pain, but the fact is, there are never any guarantees when it comes to life. Or love. We risk our hearts every time we open them, and believe me, this child will throw yours wide open. And honestly? It seems to me like Lance has, too."

"Yeah," I admit. "He has." Images of his handsome face flash in front of my eyes. I pick up my phone and stare at it. Should I call him? Tell him I'm coming back? Maybe he's too angry to take me back.

That thought stabs me straight through my gut.

"I miss my friends, too," I realize aloud. Tabitha, Sadie and Adele are like sisters to me now. If it takes a village to raise a child, they would have been my village. Why would I move away from that?

"I think you had a trauma. Getting kidnapped scared you and set fire to your worries over creating the perfect life for your children. It made you want to run and hide in a hole, so you came here. We must've done something right if your safe place is still with us."

I let out a watery laugh. "Yeah, I guess you're right."

But my safe place isn't still with them. I just thought it was. My safe place is with Lance.

All the time I was kidnapped, when I was freaking out, I just kept thinking that he would come and save me. Of course, he did. And when things went wrong on the rescue, and it looked like we were going to die, he saved me again. Easily. With a smile. Lance isn't afraid.

He isn't human— he doesn't have the same fears I do.

But he does have needs. And he told me that one of them is staying close to me—his mate—and protecting his pup.

So I did the cruelest thing possible in leaving him. Taking away his family. How could I be so thoughtless?

I rub my head, and my mom pats my shoulder. "Get some rest. You'll feel better after a nap."

I trudge back to bed, and curl up around a big pillow. I've only closed my eyes for a few minutes when my mom sticks her heads into my room. "Charlie? There's someone out here to see you."

What? Who would come visit me here? I don't know anyone in Arizona, other than my folks. "Who?" I slide off my bed. Maybe Tabitha, Adele and Sadie made a road trip— but Adele is still dealing with the fallout from her business partner's death, and I told Sadie and Tabitha privately to stay to support her. But jumping in a car to do a crazy road trip is something Tabitha would do.

"Just come see." My mom walks away and I scramble after her.

"Did they say what they wanted?"

"No." My mom squints at me, looking amused. "Charlie, did you order a new car?"

"What?" I quicken my steps and head to the door. My mom is right. In the driveway is a shiny, silvery blue minivan. Brand new. There's even a red bow on the front.

"My god." I walk barefoot down the drive. The minivan is bigger up close. A boat-sized monstrosity, designed to haul kids and dogs with optimum safety. A soccer mom's fantasy. No sign of who brought it.

There's a beep, and I jump as the minivan's passenger doors glide open. There are two brand new car seats in the back. One is designed for a baby, the other for a toddler. I know this because I've been shopping online for car seats. A stroller rolls out from behind the car—light blue to match the car seats. Pushing the stroller is Lance. "Hey, baby."

My jaw drops to the pavement.

"Check this out." He rolls the stroller up to the baby car seat, and unhooks the top part somehow. "If the baby's napping and we want to get her in or out of the car..." A click, and he sets the baby car seat backwards on the stroller. "Easy peasy." The matching stroller and car seat become one. Lance lifts the whole thing easily to show me. "It's called the all-in-one baby travel system."

I find my voice. "I know. I have one in my online shopping cart. Lance, what are you doing here?"

He straightens. His blond hair is mussed and his face looks leaner, almost gaunt. He dips his head to catch my eyes, looking a little uncertain. But his eyes flare when they catch mine.

"Delivering your new car seats." He prowls up the driveway, sexy as ever. He stops a few feet away, his hands outstretched, forearms and biceps taut and quivering a little, as if he wants to reach out and pull me into his arms. I kind of wish he would. I didn't realize how amazing it would feel to see him. Lance is more than my baby-daddy. He might be it for me.

"I had to see you," he says. His voice is raspy, like he hasn't had a drink of water in a long time. "You look good."

"Thanks," I whisper. I realize I have my hands on my belly and drop them to my sides. "What is this?" I nod to the minivan.

"Your new ride." The corner of his mouth turns up as he gives the car a rueful smile. "Isn't she pretty?"

"She's big."

He chuckles. "Not exactly my dream ride, either, but it's what you need. And if you like it, I'm going to buy one for me, too."

"What!"

Behind me, the front door closes. My mom leaving me to my fate. I don't care.

"Lance, you can't do that." I take a few steps and now I'm the one leaning forward, my body tense and vibrating, ready to leap into Lance's arms.

"Already done," he says gently. He takes a step forward. Hesitates. "I know I'm not what you would choose," he says, "but I want you to know that I choose you. Charlie, I choose you over everything."

Tears prick my eyes. "So what does that mean?"

"Here's your new minivan. Stroller. Car seats." He gestures to each in turn. "Did you know the fire department will teach you how to put car seats in? I stopped at six fire departments, and now I'm a pro." He sounds proud. "And look…" He walks around the car and pushes a button. The trunk door glides open and my mouth gapes wider. Stacked in the back are boxes and boxes of diapers. All types. All sizes. Each box has pictures of chubby, happy babies and toddlers crawling on the sides. "And I got wipes." Lances reaches in and pats the row of boxes in the back. "In bulk. Apparently, we're going to need a lot of them." He shrugs his broad shoulders.

"You got a minivan." I still can't wrap my head around it. I have a panicky thought. "Lance you didn't... You didn't sell the Ducati, did you?"

Now both corners of his mouth turn up. "I would have, baby. I left it in Taos. Put it in storage. Figured you might want to ride again someday." He steps closer, wheeling the stroller to the side so there's nothing but a few feet of air between us. "But if not, Charlie, it's okay. I can give it up. I can give up anything. The only thing I can't live without on this planet is you."

I stare at him, heart pounding. The world narrows and all I see is Lance's beautiful face.

A loud honk makes me jump. A black BMW convertible has pulled up to the curb. Out pops a woman wearing a blush pink pantsuit and a broad smile. "Hello!" She waves, pulling off her oversized Ray-Bans. "I'm Amy. It's so nice to meet you! Lance? And you must be Charlie!" The sun glints off her extra white teeth, blinding me. "I'm your new realtor!" She splays her hands like she's expecting confetti to fall from the sky.

"Um..." I stare at Lance.

"Hey, Amy. Thanks for coming out." Lance nods to her.

"Of course! I have, like, five homes for us to see today." Amy digs a folder out of her huge purse and waves it at us. "Are you guys ready to go?"

What? I mouth to Lance. I feel like I've been dropped

into a prime time family sitcom. The only thing missing is my parents popping out the front door to a laugh track.

"Yeah," Lance says, rubbing the back of his neck. "Can you give us a moment?"

"Of course," Pantsuit Amy chirps, and pivots on her nude pumps. She heads back down the driveway, pulling out her phone.

"A realtor, Lance?"

"Yeah, I figured I'd better get a move on settling into a place nearby. Was hoping you'd come look at some places with me. Give me your opinion. Oh, and," he ducks into the front seat and grabs a sheet of paper, "here's a list of the best places to give birth." He hands me the printout. "There are some hospitals on there and OB-GYNs. But also a birthing center that came highly recommended. Kylie helped me make the list." He swipes a hand over his forehead, eyeing me. "I know you're doing your own research, but I wanted to help."

"Wait." I can't process all this. I glance from the paper, to the minivan, to Pantsuit Amy. "Are you moving here?"

Lance steps close. So close, my cells cry out for him to touch me. But he leaves a few inches between us as he murmurs, "I told you, Charlie. You're it for me. And I don't want another second to go by where we're more than a town apart." He swallows hard, his Adam's apple bobbing. "I mean, I'd rather you be in my bed," he purrs. Heat flares between my legs. "But if not, I can deal. I figured I could buy a house close to your folks. Or maybe a duplex? You can live on one side; I'll live on the other. We can share the backyard."

There's a knot in my throat the size of a minivan. "Lance, you can't just leave Taos. What about your pack?" I add in a low voice, glancing to make sure the realtor can't hear. She's walking around the cul-de-sac, chatting on her phone. The blinds over my mom and dad's front bay window are still, but I bet my mom is peeping through a crack. We definitely have an audience.

I step closer to Lance so I can whisper, not because I'm dying to touch him. "Are you really moving here?"

"I told you, Charlie." His murmur caresses my ears. "You're the only one I need."

And then I can't wait any longer. I take two steps and launch myself into his arms. He's there to catch me. Like always.

"Lance," I cry, wrapping my legs around him. He feels so good between them. Like always.

"Baby." He's kissing my face and my neck, licking and nipping a little too. We're giving the realtor and my parents a show, and I don't even care.

"I'm sorry if I hurt you. I didn't mean to, I just was freaked out. I know it was pretty rash thinking I could just up and move here."

He makes a noncommittal sound. "I might have been a little rash, too."

"This isn't rash," I tell him. "This is perfect." I'm crying fresh tears now, but this time they're happy tears. "You came for me. With a minivan!" I shower his face with kisses.

"What do you say, baby?" He nips my ear, his palms on my ass, squeezing hard. "You want to let me in? You want to do this together? Birthdays, first day at kindergarten, Little League games? I'm willing to do it for our kid, but I'd rather do it with you."

"Oh my God, yes. Yes."

Lance sets me down gently and goes to one knee and pulls out a pacifier. "Will you be my baby-mama?"

I swat his shoulder. "I'm already your baby-mama."

"Let's make it official, then." He slides the ring on the

back of the pacifier onto my right ring finger. Then reaches into his pocket and pulls out a real ring, sparkling with a line of yellow gems. My birthstone. The real ring fits perfectly on my left ring finger. It's different. Unique. Just like us.

I lean down and kiss him.

"OMG!" The realtor streaks up the driveaway, holding out her phone and clicking a picture. "Did he just propose? I'm so happy to be here during this special time!"

This is worse than restaurant staff who insist on singing happy birthday. I mouth to Lance: *Get rid of her.*

"Uh, Amy, can you come back another time?" Lance calls over his shoulder, wincing as she snaps another photo.

"Of course!"

I muffle my laugh against Lance's shoulder as the click of heels tells me she's walking away.

"Sorry, baby. Overkill."

"It's okay." I smooth his hair back. "It's just, we won't be needing a realtor at all. I don't want to move here."

He cups my cheek. "You sure, baby? I'll do whatever you want."

"Lance…" My voice hitches. He's beautiful and he's here, warm and solid against me. I'm drowning in his ocean eyes. "I'm sure. You're the one for me. I realized that before you showed up."

"Don't cry, Charlie." Lance kisses away a tear.

"It's hormones." I laugh through my tears, holding his face and kissing it, and he turns me in slow circles. "And I'm sure. I want you to take me back to Taos. I miss my other family."

"Yeah? You sure?" He walks me toward the new minivan and pins my ass against it, pressing into me.

"I'm sure. I made a huge mistake. I missed you so much.

And I was wrong about your work. Your missions don't make me vulnerable. They make us safe."

"I quit," he tells me. "You were right. I have Little League to coach. And I was thinking about becoming a CPA or something."

"Stop it!" I laugh, even as my heart aches with how perfect he is. "I don't want you to quit. I mean, not for me. You don't need to change anything for me. I was out of my mind when I didn't think you were the perfect man. I mean, *mate*. You're the one, Lance. It's you, all the way."

Lance flashes that pirate grin at me and slides his lips across mine. "It's you all the way for me, too," he murmurs.

A loud throat-clearing sounds from behind us and Lance whirls, expertly lowering me to my feet just before he sticks out his hand. "Lance Lightfoot, sir." He's instantly the soldier, his chest lifted, shoulders back. He's as respectful and as respectable as they come.

My dad grudgingly takes his hand and shakes it. "I'm Ed Holland. Minivan, huh?"

"Yes, sir. I thought I'd better get a family-friendly vehicle. You know, for carpool and Little League."

My dad's lips actually quirk at that. "Sounds reasonable."

"Yes, sir. And I thought I came down here to house-hunt with Charlie, but it sounds like I'll be taking her back up to Taos with me."

My mom appears behind my dad, beaming at us both. "I think that's the best thing," she says. "Not that I didn't want to have my grandchild close. I'm Sandra Holland." She extends her hand to shake Lance's.

"Lance Lightfoot."

"I'm glad you came for Charlie," my mom says.

"Always," Lance says, sliding a look my way. "I will always come for Charlie."

harlie

"I CAN'T BELIEVE you got me a minivan." I clutch Lance's neck as he carries me across the threshold of a suburban rental house on the quiet end of a cul-de-sac. I love my mom and dad but I'm glad Lance booked his own place. We're spending one night here before heading back to Taos. It was either that or tear off each other's clothes in my parents' driveway.

"You mean I got *us* a minivan." Lance maneuvers the door shut without putting me down. The place is fully furnished and quiet, with cream walls and wall to wall carpeting. With an intent look on his face, Lance marches through the house.

"You don't have to carry me, you know. I'm pregnant, not an invalid."

"That's not what your mom told me." He fixes me with a stern look. Mom told him all about my morning sickness.

More like all-day-sickness. Our first stop after leaving my parents' house was to a health food store to stock up on natural anti-nausea remedies. Lance bought me every type of candied ginger. It seems to be working.

"Lance, I'm fine." The truth is, I haven't felt nauseated since I saw him, though the candied ginger was delicious.

He growls, shouldering open the door to the master bedroom. There's a king-sized four-poster bed dominating the room, and he heads right to it. A hunter catching sight of his quarry. He's so sexy, I can't help run my hand over his blond scruff. He turns his head and nips my palm. My pussy pulses in response.

"You say you're fine. I'm gonna make sure." He lays me out on the bed, letting me down slowly. Like I'm made of glass. A treasure he'll handle with care.

His gentleness makes me blink back tears. Again. Drat these hormones.

"You're the most important thing in the world to me." He holds himself over me, sliding his stubbled jaw along my face as he whispers in my ear. "I'm gonna prove it to you."

"You bought the most uncool car on Earth and drove it willingly. After filling it with boxes of diapers. And you practiced putting diapers… on a doll." I crack up. I can still see his face when I found the real-life baby doll swaddled in a newborn-sized diaper.

"Shit," Lance mutters. "You tell anyone about that…"

"Don't worry. Secret's safe with me." I love that he was practicing, but I can imagine how his pack would tease him. "My point is, you don't have to prove anything. You've done enough."

"No, Charlie." He draws back, his thumb rubbing my cheek. "I've only begun."

I hook my arms around his neck and pull him down on

top of me but he breaks the kiss and sits back. He tugs off my shoes and socks, raising my leg to kiss my ankle. I squirm.

"Lance." I reach for him but he takes my wrists, kissing the pulse point on each before pressing them to the bed on either side of me.

"Stay." He pins me with his cerulean gaze as he slides a large hand under my shirt. His palm splays over my midriff, pausing to cup my belly. His gaze turns so tender, I tear up again.

"Lance," I whisper.

"That's right, angel, say my name." He pulls up my shirt to kiss my belly. "I'm going to take care of you," he promises my belly button.

I sniffle because he's talking to our baby.

"I'm going to take care of you," he repeats to me, lifting his head. I'm drowning in his ocean blue eyes. He climbs over me, holding his hard body above mine. He kisses my mouth, his tongue sweeping inside and thrusting, dominating. I arch into him and he locks my wrists above my head, taking control. His mouth sears mine and moves on, planting kisses on each side of my lips and along the line of my jaw. He peppers kisses in a methodical rhythm all the way up to my ear.

"Arms up," he orders and draws my shirt over my head. His hands reach behind me and unhook my bra with the deftness that can only come with practice. *Such a player.* But now he's mine.

He cups my breasts, his thumbs stroking around the areolas. The sensation zings from my nipples to my pussy. I'm restless, arching my back, trying to push my chest further into his palms. Lance's cheek curves. He settles down, nuzzling between the swollen mounds.

"These are going to get bigger for me soon," he says

absently, and scrapes his stubble into my cleavage before soothing the roughened skin with his tongue. He plants kisses over every pale inch until my belly clenches. Then he draws back. "I'm going to take care of you too," he promises each nipple. I roll my eyes.

Lance rears back, catches my hip with a casual hand, and flips me onto my stomach. The movement is swift but he steadies me. "You okay?"

"Yeah." I'm breathless. My butt tingles as he passes a hand down it. I feel the warmth of his palm through my jeans. His hand claps my bottom. "Behave." He kisses between my shoulder blades, his stubble prickly on my skin. He rubs his chin against it, making me squeal, then kisses away the rough sensation. He reaches around and undoes my jeans. I don't know how he deals with skinny jeans so easily but he peels them right off and then tugs my underwear up, baring my butt. He cups each cheek, squeezing.

"You going to take care of my ass, too?" I snark, my mouth half-muffled by the comforter.

"Maybe." He grips my right cheek harder, and dips his thumb under my flimsy panties, into my crease. I clamp my cheeks together. He chuckles and doesn't push it. He leans down to give my butt a bristly kiss. "So perfect. My Charlie." He hooks his hands on either side of my panties and jerks outwards, and they fall away, and now I'm naked and he's not. But when I reach for him, he shakes his head. "Uh-uh. You're not in charge. Lie back and put your arms over your head."

"Or else what?" I wrinkle my nose at him, even though I'm already doing as he says.

"Or you get none of this." He scrunches up his t-shirt, showing his gorgeous abs. There's the faintest blond happy trail leading right into his jeans…

Fuck. He's bluffing but I don't want to call it. Plus, the sooner I do this, the sooner I get what I want. I lie back quickly and lift my arms over my head, arching my back. I'm naked and on display. Desire stabs my belly, pulling a whimper from me, curling my toes.

Lance leans down beside the bed, rummaging around for something, and then lifts up a coiled band of purple rope.

"You know, Charlie," he says as he unwinds the rope slowly, "moving to Green Valley was a very impulsive thing to do. Very out of character for my little planner." He arches a blond brow.

I search for an answer, but I've got nothing. I'm too busy trying not to hyperventilate from arousal.

"Don't worry, angel." He bends down to murmur against my lips, "You don't have to plan anything ever again. I'm in charge."

Mini orgasm.

I never knew how hot it could be to watch someone tie me up. I lie quietly as Lance leans over me, propping me the way he wants. He kisses my palm before winding the rope around my wrists. Within seconds, I'm trussed with my arms above my head, tied to the sturdy mahogany headboard. I look up at the ceiling and wiggle my toes.

"Four-poster bed," I murmur. "Convenient."

Lance winks and sets the rope down at the foot of the bed. And then I realize it wasn't convenient. It was planned. He thought of everything, and that is so hot. I can lie back and give in to pleasure.

"Comfortable?" he asks, grasping my foot with his hand.

I stretch a little bit, loosening my shoulders. "I'm good." My naked body is stretched out like a virgin's on an altar. Lance walks to the end of the bed, where the bed posts frame him. He slowly draws up his shirt and lets it drop. His dick presses against the seam of his jeans. I lick my lips, but he only undoes the button of his jeans, nothing else, before coming around to test the ropes holding my arms.

He tugs each one, then runs one finger down my inner arm. It tickles but I can't move or do anything about it. *Damn, that's hot.* He settles between my legs and I arch my back, pushing my breasts up further so they're on display. He licks at them, then kisses a path down my belly to my pussy. I jerk, and he growls at me. "If you don't stay still, I'll make you."

Oh fuck. Three more nuzzling kisses to the inside of my right thigh and I'm squirming so much, he picks up the rope. He grabs my ankles and gently tugs me down the bed. This time he uses leather cuffs around my ankles, attaching the rope to the D-rings and knotting the other ends to the lower bed posts.

"Such a Boy Scout," I murmur, watching him finish an intricate knot.

"Not quite." His canines flash with his grin, and the mark he gave me throbs in response. *I'm his marked mate.*

"What would you have done?" My voice wavers a little as I ask. "At my parents' house... if I had said no?"

"I would have given you that sweet minivan," he says, leaving the rope and crawling over me. He holds himself on his taut biceps as I quiver under him. "And then I would have stalked you every day and night. You would have been seeing a wolf everywhere you turned."

I'm panting now. I'm the wolf's prey, caught fast. "You wouldn't let me go, would you?"

"Never," he breathes. He reaches under me to stroke my mark. Pleasure sparks through me, and I cry out. Orgasming, just like that.

He draws back to watch my face. "That wasn't part of the plan."

"You have a plan?" Why is that so sexy?

"Mmm hmm." He dips his head, nuzzling at my neck, and sensation sparkles from my core all the way down my limbs. "This is how it's going to go. I'm going to spend some time getting reacquainted with your beautiful body, and you're going to lie there and take it."

Oh God.

"Am I going to like this?" I try to tease, but I'm already breathless. He kisses down my neck, returning to my breasts, stopping at my collarbone.

"Some of it," he says. "But I think you deserve a little punishment for not calling me the moment you knew you wanted me back."

"I was working up the nerve. I was afraid you were mad at me, and I felt terrible for hurting you…"

"I know. It's okay." He kisses my jaw softly, thumbs stroking the inner curve of my hips in maddening rhythm. I try to move so I can get more stimulation on my pussy, but the ropes bind me tight. His grin turns wicked. "This is what happens when you run from a wolf. You're my mate, Charlie. I'll hunt you to the ends of the earth."

Lance

Charlie's stretched out before me, a buffet of soft skin I can lick and nibble. I have her legs splayed and tied apart. Her pussy perfumes the room, and damn if my mouth isn't watering. My dick throbs hard enough to burst out of my jeans. But it's not time to fuck my mate yet. First, I need to:

1. Tease Charlie until she's close, then back off
2. Repeat until she's begging
3. Slam my dick into her and make her scream

Stand down, I tell my wingman. Gotta stick to the plan. But damn, it's hard. The little noises she makes as I browse over her breasts, the way her chest heaves when I kiss down to her pussy, the slickness of her tight little folds, all swollen pink for me... It's super fucking hard.

Course, my dick's always hard around Charlie.

"You like this, angel?" I murmur, taking a break from licking up her nectar. "You want to come?"

"Yes, please," she groans. Her tanned skin shines with sweat. Her body's taut, her fingers clutching the ropes.

I hum and rub my jaw along the inside of her thigh, smearing her juices along her skin. Then I lick it up. Fuck, I could eat her forever.

"Please, Lance," she keens. "*Pleasepleaseplease-pleaseplease.*"

My mate sounds distressed. No good. Gotta keep baby-momma happy.

"I had a plan," I tell her as I rise up and undo the cuffs around her ankles. With her legs free, I can cup her bottom. I lift her so the head of my dick brushes her sopping entrance. "But you know what? Fuck the plan." I drive into the tight fist of her perfect cunt.

Fireworks explode behind my eyes. Her inner muscles kiss along my cock, her whole body shuddering in explosive orgasm. I watch her jerk, waiting until she draws breath, then I pull out and slam into her, setting off another wave of convulsions.

"I've got you, Charlie." I brace myself on my right arm and keep stroking smoothly into her tight heat. My left hand cups her breast, plumping and squeezing.

I tried to be patient. I tried to go slow. But my beautiful mate is tied up and begging for my dick. What was I supposed to do? Besides, she likes it when I lose control.

Charlie sighs, her eyelashes fluttering. "God yes, fuck me." Pink blooms on her chest, proof of her climaxes. The hair at her temples is damp. One wet tendril curls into an adorable ringlet. It's so precious, I twine it around my finger, slowing my thrusts. Will our baby be blond like us? Will he or she have little ringlet curls?

Fuck, Charlie's carrying our child. The thought sets me off again, and I snap my hips, driving deep. I wanna plant a baby in my mate all over again. "Come for me, angel. Come again."

Her head thrashes back and forth as she fights her climax. The keening sound hums in her throat. I angle myself over her, making sure my lower belly rubs her pubic bone with each thrust. "Come," I order.

"Oh God!" In the grip of orgasm, her body strains, arching off the bed.

I need her touching me. I grab the rope above her head with both hands and jerk, pulling it apart. I free her hands and she grabs my back, her palms sliding over the sweat-slick muscles.

"Hang on," I tell her. Her pussy clenches on my dick at my order. "You like that, Charlie? You like me in charge?" Pressure builds in my head. My cock's ready to blow.

"Yes," she whimpers.

"You want me to tie you up? Take control?" I plunge deep and swivel my hips. Her nails dig into my back. "You're going to come for me, angel. One more time."

"No…"

"You can do it. I've got you. We'll go together."

Her eyes fly to mine. "Together," she whispers.

I hold her eyes and bow my back so I can murmur against her lips, "It's a plan."

She grabs my head and smashes her mouth against mine.

And we go over like that, clutching each other close. For a while we're lost in each other, kissing and catching our breath. Then I rise up to check the ropes. She has a few marks on her wrists and ankles from straining against her bonds. Nothing too dramatic. I kiss them and she shudders happily.

At least I didn't wreck the bed. The posts might have some rope marks on them. I'll have to pay the rental owner to get the bed replaced.

I clean up, and go to run a bath. Charlie smiles drowsily at me when I return, so I carry her and sit down in the bath with her right in my lap. The water's warm but not too warm. Charlie's bottom brushes over my cock—it loves that. I grit my teeth and concentrate on cleaning her up while she sprawls, boneless, against my chest.

"I can't believe you did this," she murmurs, blinking up at me. She's so worn out, she looks drunk. Drunk on pleasure. "I can't believe you came all the way to Green Valley."

"It's you and me, Charlie. For the rest of our lives." I scoop her out of the bath and dry her off. She sways against me, yawning, and I carry her to the bedroom and get us into bed. I pull her against me and tug the sheet over us. My wolf sighs. My mate's back in my arms.

"You're going to be the sexiest Little League coach ever," she mumbles.

"Go to sleep, angel. I've got you." I lock my arms around her, drawing her into the protection of my body. Where she belongs.

CHAPTER 18

harlie

A ROAD TRIP in a minivan is a lot more fun that I would have thought. Even with a trunk full of boxes of diapers. Lance drives and I sit in the front seat, a bag of candied ginger on my lap.

"Almost home," Lance says, turning into my neighborhood. We've decided to move in together. I love my home, and so does Lance. I've already made plans to transform my office into a nursery. Lance has a big honey-do list to work on the next few months. The first priority: adding places to my bed frame where he can secure rope. Lance is most excited about that project.

"Home, sweet home." Lance slows the car as we approach my house.

"What the…" My mouth drops open. My house looks… different. For one thing, there are baby blue and pink streamers covering the roof. Channing and Deke are up there, tying enough balloons to the chimney to make it float away.

Rafe's on the ground, hand shading his eyes. I can't hear but I can tell he's shouting up orders. Next to him, taking up most of the lawn, is a giant inflatable thing—the sort you see at Halloween. Only this is a baby blue teddy bear. Its head is up near the roof. Channing looks like he wants to jump on it.

My front door opens and my friends pour out. Sadie carries more balloons, puffy gold ones that spell 'BABY'. She sees us and waves, bouncing up on her ballet flats while Tabitha and Adele turn to look up at Channing, who's pretending he's going to leap from the roof onto the inflated bear. Tabitha laughs but Adele shakes her head, putting her hands on her hips. Now Channing's getting chewed out by both Rafe and Adele.

"Looks like someone planned a surprise baby shower." I twist towards Lance. "Did you plan this?"

"Nope." He grimaces. "You want me to take you back to Arizona?"

"Nope. I can deal. I like surprises." I put a hand on his knee. "Especially when I'm with you."

"Damn straight." He leans over to kiss me.

I pretend to draw away. "Think of the children," I say in a fake-shocked voice, glancing into the backseat. I buckled the baby doll in the infant car seat, promising Lance I'll tell everyone it's mine. I may have practiced putting a diaper on it myself, though Mom tells me it's a lot different diapering a living, squirming child.

"They'd better get used to it," Lance growls and cups the back of my neck. His kiss is long and deep and sets my pussy tingling—until someone honks a horn. I jerk back, and Lance glares out at our friends. Rafe has his arms crossed but he's smiling. Tabitha's leaning into her bright yellow VW bug. She's the one honking the horn.

"My friends are nuts." I shake my head.

"My pack is worse," Lance counters. He parks and hops out, jogging around to my door and opening it for me. The sight of his sexy self, framed in the door of a clumsy minivan, is enough to make my panties wet. His smirk says he knows it. "Last chance, angel. We can ditch these guys; hit the road."

"Nope, I'm done running."

"Then let's do this. Ready?" He holds out his hand.

"Ready." I take it and we walk together up my drive, to our future with friends and packmates, and the love we'll share for the rest of our lives.

MEET CHARLIE and Lance's baby! Click here to read the bonus scene and join the Bad Boy Alpha newsletter.

Thank you for reading Alpha's Vow! If you enjoyed it, we would appreciate your recommendations and reviews—they mean so much to indie authors. Want more? Find out what happens when Rafe and Adele fight their attraction in *Alpha's Revenge.*

WANT FREE BOOKS?

Go to http://subscribepage.com/alphastemp to sign up for Renee Rose's newsletter and receive a free books. In addition to the free stories, you will also get special pricing, exclusive previews and news of new releases.

Download a free Lee Savino book from www.leesavino.com

Paranormal

Bad Boy Alphas Series

Alpha's Temptation

Alpha's Danger

Alpha's Prize

Alpha's Challenge

Alpha's Obsession

Alpha's Desire

Alpha's War

Alpha's Mission

Alpha's Bane

Alpha's Secret

Alpha's Prey

Alpha's Sun

Shifter Ops

Alpha's Moon

Alpha's Vow

Alpha's Revenge

Wolf Ranch Series

Rough

Wild

Feral

Savage

Fierce

Ruthless

Untamed

Wolf Ridge High Series

Alpha Bully

Alpha Knight

Midnight Doms

Alpha's Blood

His Captive Mortal

Alpha Doms Series

The Alpha's Hunger

The Alpha's Promise

The Alpha's Punishment

Other Paranormal

The Winter Storm: An Ever After Chronicle

Contemporary

Chicago Bratva

"Prelude" in Black Light: Roulette War

The Director

The Fixer

"Owned" in Black Light: Roulette Rematch

The Enforcer

Vegas Underground Mafia Romance

King of Diamonds

Mafia Daddy

Jack of Spades

Ace of Hearts

Joker's Wild

His Queen of Clubs

Dead Man's Hand

Wild Card

Daddy Rules Series

Fire Daddy

Hollywood Daddy

Stepbrother Daddy

Master Me Series

Her Royal Master

Her Russian Master

Her Marine Master

Yes, Doctor

Double Doms Series

Theirs to Punish

Theirs to Protect

Holiday Feel-Good

Scoring with Santa

Saved

Other Contemporary

Black Light: Valentine Roulette

Black Light: Roulette Redux

Black Light: Celebrity Roulette

Black Light: Roulette War

Black Light: Roulette Rematch

Punishing Portia (written as Darling Adams)

The Professor's Girl

Safe in his Arms

Sci-Fi

Zandian Masters Series

His Human Slave

His Human Prisoner

Training His Human

His Human Rebel

His Human Vessel

His Mate and Master

Zandian Pet

Their Zandian Mate

His Human Possession

Zandian Brides

Night of the Zandians

Bought by the Zandians

Mastered by the Zandians

Zandian Lights

Kept by the Zandian

Claimed by the Zandian

Stolen by the Zandian

Other Sci-Fi

The Hand of Vengeance

Her Alien Masters

Regency

The Darlington Incident

Humbled

The Reddington Scandal

The Westerfield Affair

Pleasing the Colonel

Western

His Little Lapis

The Devil of Whiskey Row

The Outlaw's Bride

Medieval

Mercenary

Medieval Discipline

Lords and Ladies

The Knight's Prisoner

Betrothed

The Knight's Seduction

The Conquered Brides (5 book box set)

Held for Ransom (out of print)

Renaissance

Renaissance Discipline

ALSO BY LEE SAVINO

Paranormal romance

The Berserker Saga and Berserker Brides (menage werewolves)

These fierce warriors will stop at nothing to claim their mates.

Draekons (Dragons in Exile) with Lili Zander (menage alien dragons)

Crashed spaceship. Prison planet. Two big, hulking, bronzed aliens who turn into dragons. The best part? The dragons insist I'm their mate.

Bad Boy Alphas with Renee Rose (bad boy werewolves)

Never ever date a werewolf.

Tsenturion Masters with Golden Angel

Who knew my e-reader was a portal to another galaxy? Now I'm stuck with a fierce alien commander who wants to claim me as his own.

Contemporary Romance

Royal Bad Boy

I'm not falling in love with my arrogant, annoying, sex god boss. Nope. No way.

Royally Fake Fiancé

The Duke of New Arcadia has an image problem only a fiancé can fix. And I'm the lucky lady he's chosen to play Cinderella.

Beauty & The Lumberjacks

After this logging season, I'm giving up sex. For...reasons.

Her Marine Daddy

My hot Marine hero wants me to call him daddy...

Her Dueling Daddies

Two daddies are better than one.

Innocence: dark mafia romance with Stasia Black

I'm the king of the criminal underworld. I always get what I want. And she is my obsession.

Beauty's Beast: a dark romance with Stasia Black

Years ago, Daphne's father stole from me. Now it's time for her to pay her family's debt...with her body.

ABOUT RENEE ROSE

USA TODAY BESTSELLING AUTHOR RENEE ROSE loves a dominant, dirty-talking alpha hero! She's sold over a million copies of steamy romance with varying levels of kink. Her books have been featured in USA Today's *Happily Ever After* and *Popsugar*. Named Eroticon USA's Next Top Erotic Author in 2013, she has also won *Spunky and Sassy's* Favorite Sci-Fi and Anthology author, *The Romance Reviews* Best Historical Romance, and *has* hit the *USA Today* list seven times with her Wolf Ranch series and various anthologies.

Please follow her on:
  Bookbub | Goodreads

Renee loves to connect with readers!
www.reneeroseromance.com
reneeroseauthor@gmail.com

ABOUT LEE SAVINO

Lee Savino is a USA today bestselling author, mom and chocoholic.

Warning: Do not read her Berserker series, or you will be addicted to the huge, dominant warriors who will stop at nothing to claim their mates.

I repeat: Do. Not. Read. The Berserker Saga.

Download a free book from www.leesavino.com (don't read that either. Too much hot, sexy lovin').

Made in United States
Orlando, FL
03 February 2022

14393070R00146